HOT ZONE

Depth Force Thrillers
Book Fifteen

Irving A Greenfield

SAPERE
BOOKS

HOT ZONE

Published by Sapere Books.

24 Trafalgar Road, Ilkley, LS29 8HH,
United Kingdom

saperebooks.com

ISBN: 978-0-85495-019-5

POWER PLAY

SSN-S1 moved at flank speed through the frigid waters of the Bering Strait.

"Bottom, five feet," *a man at the fathometer called out.*

Commander Jack Boxer checked the bottom UWIS scan. The sea floor was strewn with huge boulders that could easily tear a gash in the boat's hull.

"Targets bearing zero five... Range, five thousand yards... Speed, ten knots... Course, three five zero," *the SO reported.*

Suddenly, the dreaded pinging of the Russian sonar filled the sub. "They're ranging on us, sir."

"Rig for depth charges," *Boxer announced over the 1MC.* "Then arm projectiles. Come to course, six zero."

"Targets incoming, five four, three six, closing fast, sir!"

"Helm, hard left. Stand by to launch."

"Helm, hard left. Standing by, sir. Bays one and two flooded. Doors open."

"All right, mister, get those babies to their target at —"

Just then a tremendous explosion shook the super ship.

"Damage control, report!"

"We're taking water, sir. Fast!"

CHAPTER 1

Commander John Sarkis signed the log, where the yeoman had entered the time he had arrived in the Control Room, and had taken over the conn from Admiral Borodine. Only after he made a quick check of the system display board and saw that all systems were green, did he finally settle into the captain's chair in front of the boat's master control console.

Sarkis was a tall, rangy man with black hair, and piercing black eyes. Because he was tired of the Navy's routine, he'd volunteered for this mission. He admired Boxer, and to a lesser degree, Borodine, though not because he thought that the man lacked the expertise that Boxer had, but because he harbored anti-Russian feelings which he managed, he thought, to skillfully conceal. Several times during his years of service, he had played cat and mouse with several different types of Russian submarines, ranging from attack to missile carrying.

But at the moment, Sarkis wasn't thinking about Borodine, he was thinking about Ilia Ioff, the Russian doctor aboard the boat, who he found very attractive, despite the fact that she was Russian. He had had a brief conversation with her in the wardroom just before he'd come on watch. He liked the soft tone of her voice, the way she smiled, and he was sure, from the way the coveralls fit her, that she had a spectacular body. The conversation went in fits of starts and stops, and was about sightseeing in and around Washington and nearby Virginia. He had almost asked her to let him be her guide. But he had decided that it would be better strategy to wait until he had another conversation with her... At least, that way he wouldn't be so obvious. The offer would seem casual, almost spontaneous.

Suddenly, the phone linking the CR with the Communication Center rang, and simultaneously a red light began to flash below it.

"Commander Sarkis, here," Sarkis said.

"Sir, we're picking up a mayday," the Communications Center Officer said. "Eighty north, one five zero east... ID's herself as the Soviet Sub Two Eight One."

"Are you in voice contact?"

"Negative."

"Try to open a voice channel," Sarkis said.

"Yes, sir," the COMMO answered.

Sarkis punched the Soviet boat's latitude and longitude into the SSN-S1's World Wide Target Computer, and in a fraction of a second, a map came up on the display screen. A flashing red circle indicated the boat's exact position. "Under the damn ice cap," he muttered, then he picked up the phone linking him to the 1MC, and said, "This is Commander Sarkis, Admiral Borodine, please return to the Control Room." He repeated his request, then put the phone down, and reestablished communications with the COMMO.

"I have voice contact," the COMMO said, "but even on extended amplification, it is just audible."

"Can't we digitize it, then put it back together again?" Sarkis questioned.

"We can try, but I don't think it will work," the COMMO answered.

"Give it your best shot."

"Yes, sir," the COMMO said.

Sarkis put the phone down, and keyed the Russian boat's last reported latitude and longitude into the NAVIGATIONAL

COMPUTER. Then he requested a course and distance display on the computer's monitor. In a fraction of a second, the computer displayed a course line on a map overlay that showed a portion of Alaska and the north coast of Siberia, and automatically gave an ETA of forty hours at the SSN-S1's present speed of thirty knots.

Suddenly Sarkis sensed someone behind him, and turned his head to the right.

"Problem?" Borodine asked, while he scanned the NAVCOMP.

"Mayday from one of your boats, Two Eight One, sir," Sarkis answered. "So far COMMO doesn't have voice contact."

Borodine's heart began to race. He knew the boat and its skipper, Comrade Captain First Class Vladimir Orlosky. The submariners in the Soviet Navy were like those in the American. They were a close-knit group…

"At our present speed, it will take —" Sarkis began, but Borodine said in a calm, flat voice, "I have the conn, Commander Sarkis."

"What?"

"Remain in the CR, please," Borodine told him, then to the helmsman, he said, "Come to new course, one five five."

"Coming to new course, one five five," the helmsman answered.

Borodine picked up the phone linking him with the COMC. "This is Admiral Borodine," he told the COMMO. Then he asked if a voice communication had been established with the Soviet boat.

"Negative, sir," the COMMO answered. "But we'll keep trying."

"Notify our HQ and the surface salvage ship that we're answering the mayday."

"Yes, sir," the officer said.

Borodine replaced the phone, then turning to Sarkis, who still occupied the captain's chair, he said, "Display the map of the Arctic bottom."

Sarkis quickly punched in the necessary computer code to bring up the map, and superimpose it on the map already displayed on the NAVCOMP's monitor.

"She's down on the Chukchi Plain, just off the continental shelf," Borodine said, as he studied the map.

"There's a two-thousand-foot bottom there," Sarkis added.

Though he'd heard him, Borodine didn't respond. He was not unaware of Sarkis's attitude toward him and the other Russian members of the crew. It had been a topic of conversation between him and several of his officers. He and Boxer had also discussed it, and Boxer had simply told him, "Old ideas die hard." But as far as he was concerned, a mayday was a mayday, and the rule that guided all mariners should have guided Sarkis. He should have immediately alerted the entire boat that it was responding to a mayday, regardless of his own feelings...

Borodine said, "Go to flank speed, Commander."

"Going to flank speed," Sarkis answered, turning the dial on the Master Control Console that governed the speed of the boat.

The forty-hour ETA displayed suddenly changed to twenty-eight.

The COMMO phone rang.

Borodine picked it up and identified himself.

"This is Kahn," the voice on the phone announced. "Abort mission and return to home base."

"Negative," Borodine answered, well aware that he was speaking to the director of the CIA.

"Put Admiral Boxer on," Kahn said.

"As of now, we will not acknowledge any transmission from HQ, or from the salvage ship... Over and out," Borodine said, and he replaced the phone in its niche. Then, looking straight at Sarkis, he asked, "Any questions, Commander?"

"None," Sarkis replied, with a shake of his head.

"Take the conn," Borodine said. "Maintain present course and speed."

"Aye, aye, Comrade Admiral," Sarkis answered.

Borodine knocked twice on the door to Boxer's cabin. Then, when he was about to rap a third time, the door suddenly opened, and the boat's medical officer, Dr. Ilia Ioff faced him. "He's still sleeping," she said in a whisper.

"We have an emergency," Borodine responded. "He's needed in the CR."

"Can't you handle it, Comrade Admiral?"

"He must be told what the situation is, and make whatever decisions he thinks are necessary... Neither of us have the authority to deny —"

"That you, Igor?" Boxer asked.

"Yes... And Dr. Ioff," Borodine answered, as he reached behind the doctor, and pushed the door fully open.

Boxer sat up, planted his feet firmly on the deck, and said, "Com'on in." Then, he asked, "How long did I sleep?"

Ioff answered, "A full sixty hours."

"I needed that," Boxer said, as he stood up. "But now I need a shave, a shower, and something to eat."

"Jack, the COMC picked up a mayday... A Russian boat, the Two Eight One —"

"Oh no!" Ioff gasped.

"You're responding, aren't you?"

"Yes. I ordered a change of course and flank speed," Borodine said.

"ETA?"

"Approximately twenty-eight hours."

"Has HQ been notified?"

Borodine nodded. "Kahn ordered us to remain on course. I told him we would not answer any more transmissions from HQ, or send them."

Boxer raised his eyebrows, then guffawed. "Kahn and the others must be going up the wall."

"We're the closest to them, and still we may be too late to do anything," Borodine said.

"Voice contact?"

Borodine shook his head. Then he said, "There's over a two-thousand-foot bottom where they are."

"We've been down that deep and deeper, haven't we? And in some very difficult situations," Boxer said.

Borodine nodded.

"Maybe they'll have the same kind of luck," Boxer told him in a soft, gentle voice. Then he looked at Ioff, nodded, and said, "Thank you for taking care of me."

"You still need rest," she answered.

"What I need doesn't count, doctor... That way, my calling is a lot like yours... If the two of you will excuse me, I'll shave and shower... Igor, meet me in the wardroom in a half hour."

Borodine nodded, then just before he left Boxer's cabin, he said, "Commander Sarkis has the conn."

"Any problem?" Boxer asked.

"None," Borodine answered, and, after he allowed Ioff to proceed him out of the cabin, he closed the door.

CHAPTER 2

Boxer wolfed down a couple of pieces of apple pie and two cups of black coffee, while Borodine filled him in on the details of the disaster.

"You don't think it could be one of Fong Shun Un's buddies trying to lure us into a trap?" Boxer asked.

"Could be, but I don't think it is," Borodine answered. "She's down in a place that only a nuclear-driven boat could get to."

Boxer nodded, and said, "It's not likely that even his Arab friends would have access to that kind of equipment ... but until we unload the gold we have on board... Well, we must remember that if those bandits thought they had a chance, they'd take it."

"I checked COMMO before I joined you," Borodine said. "Lots of Russian traffic. Six ships on their way to the downed craft, but none of them are closer than we are, and none of them have the kind of deep water salvage equipment that we have, and all of them are surface craft."

"I don't understand —"

Borodine shrugged his broad shoulders. He was a chunkily built man with a boyish face, and steel gray, penetrating eyes. "I believe the mayday to be authentic."

Boxer left the table and helped himself to another mug of coffee from a large urn that was built into the wall of the room.

"So far, we still haven't been able to establish voice contact," Borodine said, when Boxer returned.

"This time of year, the ice is already pretty thick... Do we have any reading on that?" Boxer asked. But before Borodine could answer, he added, "I don't expect to have to surface, but it would be nice to know that we would be able to do it without having any problem."

"We'll be able to get satellite photos," Borodine said.

"There's nothing we can do until —"

The phone rang.

"I'll get it," Borodine said, leaving the table. He picked up the phone, ID'd himself, and listened. Sarkis was on the other end. After a few moments, he thanked him, put the phone back in its cradle, and returning to the table, he said, "COMMO is sure the message is coming from a continuous tape."

Boxer ran his hand across his chin. "That's bad news," he said. "Could mean that we were wrong about Fong Shun Un's friends, or it could mean that the boat is really down, and the tape by some freak accident is still playing."

"That also means that the same freak accident is allowing it to be transmitted," Borodine said.

"There's a third possibility."

"The tape is continuous, but the men aren't there to answer our signals."

"Or that they are there, but for some reason *can't* answer," Boxer said.

"I don't like any of the possibilities," Borodine said.

"Like them or not, we're going to have to deal with one of them," Boxer responded.

There was a momentary pause in the conversation. Then Boxer said, "It has been years since I slept like that."

"You still look tired."

Boxer accepted Borodine's appraisal without comment, because he was still tired.

"When we're finally back in port —"

"Something else will come up," Boxer said. "There's always something."

"It seems that way, doesn't it?"

"Well, at least you have a family to go home to," Boxer said wistfully. "That gives you something more than what you do to put bread on the table."

"Ah, so now we're down to basics!" Borodine exclaimed.

"Just stating a fact," Boxer responded.

Borodine was about to suggest that Boxer give serious thought to settling down with one woman, when Dr. Ioff entered the wardroom.

"I hope I'm not disturbing you," she said. "But it is important that each of you know my position on the subject of Admiral Boxer's health."

Boxer frowned.

Looking straight at Boxer, she said, "It is my professional opinion that you should not be involved in any operational tasks, and that you should —"

"Thank you, doctor, but I am quite capable of judging my own ability to function," Boxer said curtly.

"Yes, until you make an error that will endanger the lives of your men," she responded, just as icily. "You need rest, you need to unwind."

Suddenly speaking in Russian, Borodine said, "The more you push this man, the more he will resist."

And she answered, "He doesn't understand —"

"Thank you for your professional opinion," Boxer said. Then, looking at Borodine, he added, "*He'll* keep me from making mistakes. In a way, he has been doing that for many years."

Again switching to Russian, Borodine said, "Do not push the man... The more you push, the more he will resist. He is not like other men."

And she answered, "He is only a man, not a superman."

"In English, please!" Boxer exclaimed. "It's rude to speak in a language that the third party doesn't understand."

Before Ioff could answer, a yeoman entered the wardroom. "Excuse me, sirs," he said respectfully.

Boxer and Borodine gave him their attention.

"These are the photos you requested," the yeoman said, holding out a half-dozen photographs.

Boxer stood up and took the photographs. Then, as he handed them over to Borodine, he thanked the man. The yeoman highballed him, and he returned the courtesy.

Boxer sat down.

"Excellent quality," Borodine said, passing three of the photographs to Boxer.

Boxer studied each of the photos for several moments, then remembering that Ilia was still there, he said, "No need to worry, doctor... I take full responsibility for whatever happens to me."

"And will you take the same responsibility for *whatever happens to your crew?*" she asked.

This time he glared at her. "I always have, and I always will... Now, if you will excuse us, we have some very important matters to discuss."

"Certainly, Admiral," she answered, with an equal amount of belligerence in her tone. Then she turned and walked swiftly out of the wardroom.

Boxer smiled, and said, "She's quite a woman!"

"I would not have guessed that you thought anything about her, other than that she is meddlesome."

"Only doing her job, Admiral," Boxer said.

"Then why were you so —"

Boxer waved a finger at his friend. "Don't you start... I promise to apologize to her."

"Let's look at the photographs, and determine what kind of a situation exists on the surface."

Each picture had several numbers in its lower right corner. One set gave the exact latitude and longitude, in degrees, minutes, and seconds, where the photograph had been taken. The second set gave the precise altitude of the satellite at the time the photographs were shot. The third set of numbers gave the weather conditions, and the fourth set gave the thickness of ice, as determined by the laser measurement. The surface ice, even though it was early in the season, was eight feet thick, and moving at three knots an hour in a westerly direction.

"If we have to get to the surface in a hurry," Borodine said, "it won't be easy."

"What's easy?" Boxer asked, straight-faced.

"I was hoping that you'd tell me," Borodine answered with an equally expressionless face.

Just before they left the wardroom, Boxer said, "I'll fill Stark in on the details of the situation."

Borodine smiled.

"What's that grin supposed to mean?" Boxer asked.

"The two of you — though he's almost old enough to be your grandfather — have been cut from the same piece of cloth."

"Maybe so," Boxer said. "But I'll tell you this: I'll never match the quality of his."

Borodine put his hand on his friend's shoulder. "He'd say the same thing about himself."

"Probably. But he'd say it because he's a genuine officer and gentleman, and I say it because I know it's true," Boxer told him, as they left the wardroom.

"Then I'll say because I know the two of you," Borodine said.

Harry T. Olsen, the newly appointed Director of the CIA, was in a rage. "That man is totally irresponsible," he fumed, as he paced the length of his office. "He has a fortune of gold aboard, and he goes chasing off to answer a mayday more than a thousand miles away." Though he'd never met Boxer, he had heard of him, and what he heard he didn't like. He believed in teamwork, and Boxer was anything but a team worker.

Seated around the coffee table were William B. Smith, Secretary of the Navy, Admiral Hays, Chief of Naval Operations, and a member of the Joint Chiefs of Staff. The three men had been summoned by Olsen to deal with the situation.

"Kahn told me about Boxer," he continued to rail. "But I also —"

"Excuse me," Hays said, "but if you checked the maps, and all of the other information, you would see that the SSN-S1 is the closest —" Hays was the only one of the three who knew Boxer. He had served with him on the old *Shark*.

"That's a Russian boat, and —"

"What happened to *glasnost*?" Hays asked.

Olsen stopped pacing. "I want you to order Boxer to return—"

"I'm afraid that can't be done," Hays said. "The SSN-S1 is not responding to our calls."

"What?"

"No doubt Boxer has ordered strict radio silence," Hays answered.

"Can he do such a thing?" Olsen asked, looking at Smith, who like himself was newly appointed to the position.

Hays answered before Smith could. "He can and has."

Olsen dropped down into the only empty chair at the coffee table. "Then you're telling me that we can't do anything to stop him?"

"Yes," Hays answered. "That's what I'm telling you."

"I want the man brought up on charges, tried, and gotten rid of," Olsen said, launching himself out of the chair.

"He's not strictly in my jurisdiction," Hays answered.

"Then who has authority over him?"

"You have some," Smith said.

Olsen was at the window, and turned around. "Some, what does *some* mean?" he demanded to know.

"Boxer is in a kind of gray area," Hays said, now taking perverse delight in annoying Olsen.

"What gray area?" he questioned, approaching the coffee table again. "He is in the Navy, isn't he?"

"Yes and no."

"Would you mind being a tad clearer, Admiral?"

"Boxer is not carried on any roster... As far as the Navy is concerned, he does not exist."

"*He does not exist,*" Olsen echoed sarcastically. "If he does not exist, who pays him?"

"I have no idea," Hays answered.

"He does wear a naval officer's uniform, doesn't he?"

"Yes... He also holds the rank of Admiral, but you will not find him, or his rank —"

"Somewhere there must be paper on him," Olsen fumed. He was a tall, naturally ruddy-looking man. But now his natural complexion was several shades redder. "You know, I'm beginning to realize that the reason why Boxer can do what he is doing, is because he knows no one knows where he belongs... Well, gentlemen, let me assure you that not only do I intend to find out where Boxer belongs, but I also intend to end his modern day buccaneering once and for all... I do not appreciate having an individual associated with this organization who is not a team player, and Boxer is certainly not a team player."

Smith nodded. Then he said, "According to what I could find out, those who serve with him have the same status that he has, unless they are TDY to him, and then it's usually to a ship that is undergoing long-term repairs at some shipyard or other."

Olsen launched himself off the chair. "Well, whatever was in the past, will not be in the future. Once our buccaneering Admiral returns, we'll either put him on our leash, or he can seek employment somewhere else."

Hays started to laugh.

"I fail to see any humor —"

"Oh, but there is... Admiral Jack Boxer is worth — though no precise figure is available — somewhere between twenty-five and fifty million dollars." He let that sink in before he continued. "Obviously, he doesn't have to worry about employment, and as for going elsewhere, the Russians would be only too glad to have him, or for that matter, any other country."

"He wouldn't dare do that."

"Probably not," Hays answered. "But if I were you, I wouldn't dare even think about putting a leash on him... You don't even think about doing something like that, unless you're a fool."

Olsen's ruddy complexion became several shades darker.

"And, of course, you're not, or you wouldn't occupy the chair behind that desk," Hays said.

For several moments, the two men glared silently at one another, each trying to outstare the other. But Olsen was the first to look away, and he said, "Admiral, I want copies of all messages from the SSN-S1."

"When we receive a message, you will be sent a copy," Hays answered.

"I see no reason to continue this meeting," Olsen said, and he started back to his desk, while Hays and Smith headed for the door.

"Just one more thing," Hays said, facing Olsen before opening the door.

Olsen, who was already scanning the papers on his desk, looked up. "And what's that?" he asked.

"A piece of information that might cause you to think twice before making a mistake."

"I'm listening."

"You may think you're in the Big League because you sit behind that desk, but Boxer *is* the Big League," Hays said.

"And what's that supposed to mean?" Olsen asked, his voice hard with anger... Hays wasn't a team man, that much was obvious.

"It's just something for you to think about," Hays said with a smile. "Something to ponder." Then he closed the door.

CHAPTER 3

Boxer studied the details of the downed boat on the monitor in his cabin. The SSN-S1 was equipped with — as were all American submarines — a database that gave them not only the vital stats on any foreign submarine and surface vessel, but also a three-dimensional cutaway, showing as much detail as our intelligence sources had available. The database was updated periodically.

The boat was twenty-five thousand tons, carried twenty ICBMs, and because it was highly automated, it carried a crew of forty enlisted men and ten officers. It could do fifty knots under water, and twenty-five on the surface.

Boxer moved the image of the boat into various planes. But nothing that he saw could give him any clue to what might have gone wrong. The boat was structurally sound, except like all the Russian nuclear submarines, it did not have the kind of redundancy built into its reactor system, though it was better protected against a runaway nuclear reaction than most of their boats.

A tap on his cabin door caught his attention. "Yes, who is it?" he called out.

"Dr. Ioff," came the answer.

"Come," Boxer said.

The door opened, and Ilia took a half-step forward. "I brought you these," she told him, holding out a small medicinal-type paper cup. "They will help you sleep."

Boxer stood up.

"Please take them," she said.

He nodded, and thanked her.

"If you need more…"

He looked down at the four small yellow capsules; then, back at her. "How many do I take?" he asked.

"I wouldn't advise taking more than one… They're very strong."

"And will I have good dreams when I sleep?" he asked.

Suddenly she smiled, and her cheeks dimpled. "That I can't promise you," she answered.

"Bad dreams then?" he questioned.

Ilia shrugged. "I hope not," she said.

"You know, *you* might not get much sleep for a while, depending on what we find," he told her.

"Yes, I'm aware of that."

He looked back at the computer, and started to explain, "I've been studying the boat's configuration, hoping —" He stopped, and opened the door wider. "Come, I'll show you," he said, gesturing for her to follow him.

She hesitated.

"I thought you might want to see what the boat looks like," he said.

"Yes, I do," she said with sudden resolution. "I do want to see." And she entered the cabin.

Boxer reached around her and, closing the door, said, "That's it on the monitor."

He moved in front of her, put the paper cup down on the desk, and pointing to the cutaway on the screen, he said, "You're looking at it from its keel, which is tilted thirty degrees to the right."

She studied the view.

"I can move it to give any view," Boxer explained, manipulating the mouse to change it to a combination bow and stern.

"What are you looking for?" she asked, facing him.

"Something that might give me a clue to what happened," he answered. "A structural flaw, perhaps?"

"And did you find one?"

Boxer shook his head, aware now of the subtle scent of her perfume.

"Do you think that —"

"Don't ask me if I think there are any survivors," Boxer said. "I couldn't even begin to think that there are, or aren't. At least not now."

"When then?"

"We'll know if and when we can establish contact, and the way it's going, that won't be until we're there." He had no intentions of telling her anything about the nature of the signal coming from the downed boat.

"For their sake and the sake of their loved ones, I hope we find all of them alive," she said in a low, sad voice.

Boxer nodded. "I hope so, too."

She looked up at him. "You really do, don't you?... I mean, you *do*!"

He nodded. And suddenly he found himself fighting down the desire to take her in his arms. Even as he pushed the idea out of his mind, he watched color come into her face, and guessed she either sensed what he was thinking, or wanted him to do it and felt guilty.

"I better be going," Ilia said.

"Yes, and again, thank you for the sleeping pills," Boxer said.

"Remember to take them," she stressed, when she reached the door.

"I will," Boxer answered, and was just about to apologize for his former attitude when he felt a mild jolt... She must have felt it, too, because the expression on her face changed: one moment it was soft and glowing, and now it was anxious.

Boxer went to the phone. But before he could pick it up, another, and more severe jolt, staggered him and knocked books off the shelf above the desk. Then as the phone rang, the klaxon sounded, sending the crew to their battle stations.

"Go to your station," Boxer snapped, and at a run, he headed for the CR.

Borodine was already there, so was Stark.

"We were hit by something," Sarkis said.

Boxer looked up at the UWIS. "Nothing shows," he commented.

"At the keel," Sarkis told him.

Boxer adjusted the UWIS to put an image of the keel line on the monitor. "Nothing," he said, after viewing the bottom of the hull for several moments.

"All systems are green," Borodine said, looking at the System Display Board.

"Scan each system separately," Boxer ordered.

"Scanning each system," Sarkis answered from the secondary control console.

Boxer switched the UWIS back to its normal scanning pattern, and made a three-hundred-and-sixty-degree sweep. Nothing. Then he changed the pattern to make a vertical sweep of ninety degrees, using the boat's center as a locus. Again, nothing!

"What we don't know, is whether or not we have any damage on the outside," Boxer said.

"The sensors show nothing," Sarkis reported, looking at the structural status board.

"That nothing jolted this boat twice," Borodine said.

Boxer moved away from the UWIS. "We can't risk having an accident on this boat... We have to take the time to make sure that we have absolute structural integrity... Surface, Commander."

"Aye, aye, sir," Sarkis answered, and sounded the signal. Then on 1MC, he said, "All hands, now here this... All hands, prepare to surface."

"Take her up slowly," Boxer said.

Sarkis reduced the boat's speed to *slow ahead*, put a two-degree angle on the diving planes, and then blew the forward and aft ballast tanks.

The SSN-S1 responded immediately. Her bow rose slightly, and she began to move toward the surface.

"All systems green," Borodine reported.

"Switching to night vision," Sarkis said, resetting several switches that filled the interior of the boat with red light, instead of the normal daylight glow.

"Passing through five hundred," Borodine said.

Boxer made two more three-hundred-and-sixty-degree sweeps with the UWIS, and saw nothing.

"COMMO reports mayday signals are much weaker," Sarkis said.

Boxer acknowledged the report with a nod.

"Four hundred feet," Borodine called out.

"Check the weather topside," Boxer ordered.

A junior officer of the watch immediately began to adjust a series of dials and reposition several switches.

"Scattered ice floes; three- to four-foot waves; computer estimated wind, eighteen to twenty knots," the officer reported.

"Doesn't anything ever go right!" Boxer exclaimed.

"Not if Peter's law is involved, and it almost always is," Sarkis answered.

Boxer shook his head… He had wanted to have a visual check of the hull, but with that kind of sea running, it would be just about impossible, if not completely impossible.

"Two hundred feet," Borodine reported.

Boxer scanned the System Operational Board… Everything was green.

Suddenly, one of the phones rang.

Sarkis answered it, listened for a few moments, and then said, "Engineering reports out of tolerance stress on propeller shaft."

Boxer's eyes focused on the system status board, where the boat's propulsion system's operating status was displayed. "System GREEN," Boxer said.

Sarkis relayed the message to the EO, listened a moment, then reported, "The EO suggests zooming in on the drive shaft."

Boxer nodded and turned several control dials, that immediately replaced all of the systems displayed on the SDB with a computer-generated three-dimensional view of the drive shaft, its gear box, and the boat's propeller.

The display showed a shaft rotation of 900 rpm. But the dialed-in rpms was 1200.

"We're fouled on something," Boxer said.

Borodine checked the SDB.

"Fishing net?" Boxer asked.

"It could be."

Boxer reduced the rpms to 800, but the shaft was revolving at 600 rpms.

"I don't want to risk bending the shaft," Boxer said.

"One hundred feet," Borodine called out.

Boxer switched on the 1MC. "Bridge detail, stand by," he said.

"Periscope depth," Borodine reported.

Boxer sounded the klaxon. Then, on the 1MC he said, "Surface surface... All hands, now hear this, we are operating on the surface."

The sail's hatch was thrown open and frigid air rushed into the CR.

"Sarkis, you have the CR," Boxer said, and motioning to Borodine, he added, "If we can, let's see what's fouling us."

Quickly the two of them put on the necessary fleece pants, boots, foul weather gear, electrically heated boots and gloves, and, finally, face masks to prevent their faces from freezing.

As soon as they were topside, they closed the hatch and braced themselves against the driving wind. The boat was rolling from side to side, and every few moments it smashed into a growler, or a growler crashed into it.

Boxer actuated the bridge Control Console, and brought the boat to FULL STOP. Then he switched on the two high-intensity searchlights, and trained them on the stern.

"Not a damn thing!" Boxer swore.

"We're going to have to put two divers out," Borodine said.

"Get one from your group, and I'll get one from mine."

Borodine switched on the 1MC. "Dimitri Zukov, report to the bridge, ready to dive," he said.

Boxer took the mike, and ordered Juris to the bridge.

In the time that it took for Zukov and Juris to come to the bridge, Boxer also assembled two details of five men to handle the divers. Each diver would have a nylon rope tied around his waist and the other end of that rope would be tied to one of the stern cleats. The five-man detail would control the line itself, according to the radioed directions from the individual diver. The divers would work as a team.

As soon as Juris and Zukov were ready, they exited the sail through its port side deck door.

Boxer and the two five-man details joined them. Boxer said, spreading his legs to counteract the rolling of boat, "I need to know what is fouling the propeller shaft, whether there's any visual damage to the shaft, or the prop, and can we get rid of the problem."

Juris and Zukov nodded, put their breathing masks on, and adjusted the flow of air into them.

"All right, go!" Boxer ordered, at the exact moment the boat's roll put its port side close to the water.

The two men left the deck, and immediately vanished into the black water. Moments later two beams of light moved, like silver gelatinous creatures, close to the surface.

Boxer switched on his hand-held radio.

"Propeller clear," Juris reported.

"Say again," Boxer answered, wanting the report confirmed.

"Propeller clear," Juris repeated.

"No damage to prop," Zukov said.

"Return to deck," Boxer ordered, switched off the radio, and opening the sail door, stepped over the coaming, and closed the door after him. Moments later he entered the CR, quickly removed his outer clothing, and stowed them in a nearby locker.

"Secure the bridge," he told Sarkis, who immediately relayed the message to Borodine.

Boxer sat down in the captain's chair, and studied the computer derived display of the shaft, its gear box, and the propeller.

"Divers on board," Sarkis said.

"Stand by to get underway," Boxer ordered.

Sarkis switched on the 1MC. "All hands, now hear this... All hands, stand by to get underway."

Borodine joined Boxer, and said, "The shaft itself could be imperfectly machined."

Boxer squinted at him. He had thought about the possibility, but dismissed it because it was, in his opinion, way out. "That might explain the two jolts," Borodine continued. "We were moving at flank."

Boxer nodded.

"And as for the difference between what is called for and the shaft output... Well, my guess is that that condition only occurs below slow ahead, or astern."

Boxer considered Borodine's explanation... It was reasonable, *if* the shaft had been imperfectly machined. He picked up a phone that would connect him directly with the EO, and as soon as the EO answered, he said, "Admiral Borodine has come up with a reasonable explanation for what we've been experiencing..." And when he finished relating it, he asked, "Can your people generate a computer model?"

"I'm sure we can, but it will take time," the EO answered.

"Do it," Boxer answered.

"Yes, sir," the EO said.

"Can you hold our speed to — say, 200 rpms below flank?" Boxer asked.

"Yes."

"We'll go with that," Boxer answered, then he said, "Let me know as soon as you have that computer model ready."

"Yes, sir," the EO replied.

Boxer put the phone down, reached over, and pressed the klaxon button twice. Then he switched on the 1MC, "All hands, now hear this… All hands, stand by to dive… Stand by to dive…"

CHAPTER 4

After the SSN-S1 reached a depth of two hundred feet, Boxer returned the conn to Sarkis, and went back to his cabin, where he dropped down on his bunk, put his hands behind his head, and closed his eyes.

That the problem had not manifested itself during the boat's shakedown bothered Boxer enough to keep him from sleeping. And given the situation, he was reluctant to take the pills Ilia had given him... He couldn't afford to risk being groggy should an emergency occur... He smiled, said aloud, "She meant well."

Boxer opened his eyes, shifted his position, and looked at the monitor on his desk. The cutaway three-quarter view of the Russian boat was still on the screen. Ordinarily, he would have gotten up and shut down the computer system, but he just didn't have the energy to overcome his inertia. He closed his eyes again, and this time, he put his right arm over them.

Boxer drifted off into a light sleep and a melange of confused dreams in which he was either in danger, or making love. And even in the dream, he laughed at the similarity between the danger of being in love and danger of having to fight for his life.

He awoke with a start, and, as he pulled his arm away from his eyes, he heard the soft rapping on the door of the cabin.

Sitting on the side of the bunk, Boxer called out, "Come."

Ilia stood in the opened doorway. "I was told you were back in your cabin," she said.

"Just taking advantage of the down time," Boxer said.

She nodded. "The emergency —"

"It wasn't really an emergency," he interrupted. Then with a smile, he added, "It's the mother hen in me."

"It's very difficult — no, impossible — to think of you as the mother-hen type," she told him.

Boxer laughed, ran his fingers through his hair, and standing up, he said, "Well, maybe more like a father hen."

"I guess I'll have to accept that," Ilia replied with a smile. "Comrade Admiral Borodine told me that the mayday signals have stopped."

"Yes," he said sadly.

"Then, there's no hope for the crew?" she asked in an equally doleful tone.

Boxer made an open gesture with his hands, took a deep breath, and said, "I don't know what to tell you."

"Your best guess would do."

"Not much chance of finding any survivors," he said.

She hugged herself, and said, "All those men ... the families of all those men!" She shook her head, and fought back the tears.

Boxer's impulse was to take her in his arms, but instead, he looked toward the monitor where the cutaway view of the boat was displayed, and reaching over to the keyboard, he quickly removed it from the screen.

"Do you think we'll be able to recover the bodies?" she asked.

"Depends on how deep the boat is, and whether or not Comrade Admiral Borodine wants us to," Boxer answered. "He may have to check with Moscow."

"Yes, I am sure that he will, regardless of his own feelings," Ilia said. "There are probably more political ramifications to this than we realize." She hugged herself again, and added, "It is so very, very sad."

For several moments, neither of them spoke. Then Ilia said, "Try to rest as much as you can."

"I will, Comrade Doctor," Boxer answered.

She smiled at him, and turned toward the half-opened door.

"Thank you for coming," Boxer said.

She stopped, faced him, and said, "You didn't think I wouldn't, did you?"

He felt her green eyes boring into him...

"Take care of yourself, Comrade Admiral... The men need you, and —" She hesitated for a fraction of moment before finishing with, "And I need you."

Before Boxer could respond, she left the cabin, and closed the door behind her. He started to go after her, but the phone rang. He stopped, went to the desk, and picking up the phone, he ID'd himself.

"Sir, we've come up with a computer model," the EO said.

"Can I have it transferred to my monitor?" Boxer asked.

"Negative... It's not the boat's network," the EO said. "We have two non-network computers down here for special situations."

"Notify Comrade Admiral Borodine, and ask him to meet me in your office in ten minutes."

"Yes, sir," the EO answered.

Boxer put the phone down, went into the bathroom, dowsed his face with cold water, vigorously dried it, and then left his cabin.

Borodine was already in the EO's office when Boxer arrived.

"I ran two separate programs on two different computers," the EO said, as he led them into a small cubicle, where the non-network computers were housed. "The result on each is identical." He pointed to the two color screens. "Watch what happens when flank speed is simulated for an extended period of time, say eight hours." And as he ran his fingers over the keyboard for one of the computers, he added, "This is with an irregularity of one ten-thousandth of an inch anywhere on the shaft."

As Boxer and Borodine watched the screen, a wavelike motion began to move across the shaft.

"Of course, this is speeded up," the EO explained.

"Then the two jolts we felt were the result of the waves hitting the main drive gear?" Borodine asked.

"Yes," the EO said.

"And the same thing happens at very low speed?" Boxer questioned.

"Yes... Watch, as I reduce the speed to 900 rpms," the EO said.

"The wave does exactly the same thing," Borodine commented.

"Have you any idea where the irregularity is?" Boxer asked.

"No, sir. The shaft will have to be removed and thoroughly checked... But the only danger is at flank and between steerage way and slow."

Boxer thanked the EO and complimented him on a job well done. Then, to Borodine he said, "We'll be able to do what we have to."

Borodine nodded and answered, "I never thought that we wouldn't."

Anthony Hale blew a cloud of cigar smoke toward the ceiling, and shifted his position in the black leather, high-back chair. He asked, "You're sure of your information?" He was a barrel-chested man, with wavy white hair and eyes like polished obsidian.

Commander William Negron, the man on the other side of the big, highly polished teak desk, answered, "Everyone in HQ is jumping up and down, because the SSN-S1 is answering a mayday coming from a Russian sub."

Hale blew another cloud of smoke out of his mouth, but this time it was directed to his right. He was the Chief Operating Officer of the Rio Oro Corporation — an international holding company whose subsidiaries were engaged in various aspects of nuclear technology from mining uranium, to the building and operation of nuclear power plants in ten different countries, including the Soviet Union.

"The question is whether the submarine is the same one spotted by our ship?" Hale said.

The Commander shook his head.

"Does that mean you don't know, or that you can't find out?" Hale asked.

"Both."

"You mean you're the only corruptible officer in the entire United States Navy?" Hale asked, delighting in watching the man squirm.

Neither spoke for a few moments, then Negron said, "If it is, then we will really have a problem."

"You mean Admiral Borodine?"

Negron shook his head. "That's only half the problem... The other half is Admiral Boxer."

"We'll let our Russian friends handle Borodine, and we'll handle Boxer."

"No one, as you put it, *handles* either one of them," Negron said.

Hale was going to throw another gibe at the man, but decided not to push him any further, and said, "Boxer has his

Achilles' heel, just like everyone else. If it's not money, it's something else."

Negron shrugged.

"You leave Boxer to me," Hale said.

"He's all yours."

"All right, now you find out if that Russian sub is the same one picked up by our ship, or if it's a different one. If it's the same —"

"It *must* be the same one, or the Russians wouldn't have advised us that they will salvage it."

Hale launched himself forward, placing his weight on his elbows, which rested on the top of the desk. "Say again," he said, still holding the cigar in his mouth.

"We — the United States — have been advised that the Russians will respond —"

"You didn't mention anything about that before," Hale said accusingly. Now the cigar was between the thumb and his forefinger.

"With them its SOP."

"SOP," he repeated in a moderate voice. Then, suddenly, he roared, "Nothing is SOP when there's even the vaguest possibility that our operations could be jeopardized! We want only those Russian ships, whose captains are in — shall we say — sympathy with our operation."

Negron fell silent.

Hale picked up a phone, punched out a twelve digit number, waited a few moments, then said, "This is Hale. I want to know what your people are doing about your downed boat."

The voice on the other end said, "Two ships are on their way. But weather conditions will prevent them from making contact."

"Will they attempt to salvage —"

"No."

"You are sure of that?"

"Absolutely certain... My orders were to locate and mark the boat's position, but not to risk any more lives in an attempt to recover the dead."

Smiling, Hale said, "Good, very good."

"Now, tell me what you intend doing to stop the SSN-S1," the voice on the other end answered.

"Oh, we'll handle Admiral Boxer," Hale said. "And I am depending on you to do the same with Borodine."

"You can be certain that we will."

"Do you think they can reach the wreck?" Hale asked.

"That's something you'll have to tell us," the voice replied. "Your technology is far superior to ours, in the area of undersea rescue and salvage."

Hale thought for a moment, then he said, "I will let you know as soon as I can. Right now, we're not in a position to say anything more."

"Is someone with you?" the voice asked.

Hale almost nodded. "We will discuss the matter later," he said, somewhat awed by the Russian's ability to sense a situation.

"Then I expect to hear from you," the man said.

"Certainly," Hale answered, and put the phone down. "The Russians are not going to make a serious salvage effort," he said, looking at Negron.

The Commander nodded.

"This, of course, is privy information, understand?" Hale said.

"I understand," Negron answered in a low voice.

"Good... Now you go back to your men and see how much more information you can get... I'll meet you at the Officer's Club at — say, seven-thirty this evening."

"Can't we meet earlier?" Negron questioned, as he stood up.

"Seven-thirty," Hale said in a steel-hard voice. "And don't keep me waiting. I don't like to be kept waiting."

Negron remained silent.

Without bothering to look up, Hale dismissed him with a perfunctory wave.

"We have the target on the scope," the Sonar Officer reported.

Boxer switched it to the sonar monitor on the SYSCON console. Borodine sat next to him in the EXO's chair.

"She's only eight hundred feet down," Boxer commented.

Suddenly the nuclear radiation light on the console began to flash red, and the klaxon sounded, sending everyone to their battle station.

Boxer ran a quick check of the entire reactor system. "Green," he said, cutting the alarm, and informing the entire crew over the 1MC that conditions were normal.

Borodine pointed to the RAD reading coming from the external probes.

"It's more than a hundred times what it should be," Boxer said.

"The boat?" Borodine questioned.

"Let's check," Boxer answered, and placed the SSN-S1 in reverse. The more the distance between it and the downed boat grew, the more the radiation diminished.

"If there was ... say, a meltdown on board ... that wouldn't explain the use of tape to send the mayday," Borodine said.

Boxer agreed, and started the SSN-S1 back on course to where the stricken submarine lay. "A meltdown would have happened quickly... There wouldn't have been time to set the tape."

Borodine scratched his head, as he watched the dosimeter needle climb.

"We'll send out an unmanned probe," Boxer said. "If there's massive structural damage — we won't attempt a rescue operation."

"I would have to notify my government of the situation," Borodine said. "For security reasons, it might want to destroy whatever is left."

Boxer nodded. "It's your boat," he said, settling the SSN-S1 a safe distance from the boat. Switching on the 1MC, he ordered the Remote Diving Sensor readied for launching.

The RDS video-imaging device was locked into the UWIS, where its pictures were translated into digital information with a range of two hundred and fifty-six shades of the primary colors and displayed on the UWIS monitor in one finely coherent color-graded image. The other instruments on board provided readings of ambient radiation levels, temperatures, and current information.

A red flashing light indicated that the RDS was ready to launch.

"Launching RDS," Boxer announced over the 1MC, as he pressed a number of black and red buttons in sequence. The six-foot-long device was actually a modified torpedo, that was either wire-controlled or controlled by sonar by either the skipper or the SO.

"You take her in," Boxer said, glancing at Borodine.

Without comment, Borodine switched the control of the RDS to a section of the SYSCON directly in front of himself. Then he said, "Thirty knots... Depth, five hundred feet ... five thousand yards."

Boxer turned to the WO, and said, "Give me a surface weather report."

"Aye, aye, sir," the lieutenant answered.

"Sir," the COMMO reported by phone, "there's heavy Russian radio traffic."

"Anything important?" Boxer questioned.

"Everything is in code," the COMMO answered.

"Do you have a translator standing by?" Boxer asked.

"Yes, sir," the COMMO responded.

"Let me know if anything interesting comes up," Boxer said, and without waiting for the customary response, he replaced the phone in its cradle.

"Sir, weather conditions on the surface are extremely bad," the lieutenant said. "Wind gusting to sixty knots, heavy movement of the pack ice to the east, and an air temperature of thirty-five below zero."

Boxer accepted the report with a nod and turned his attention to the UWIS, where the RDS was clearly visible.

"Radiation becoming more intense," Borodine said.

Boxer didn't answer. He was trying to make an educated guess about what might have happened aboard the boat that could have caused it to sink. But if there wasn't a runaway nuclear reaction...

"First pictures are coming in," Borodine said, as the UWIS screen now showed the dark mass of the boat.

"No visible damage, so far," Boxer commented.

"Slowing RAD," Borodine said, as he moved a control dial counterclockwise.

"Nothing," Boxer said.

With a nod, Borodine agreed, then he said, "I'll make three passes... That should give us the information we need about the boat's exterior condition."

The RAD made three sweeps of the downed boat; each pass provided pictures that showed structural integrity.

"There has been an internal blowout, that's for sure," Boxer said.

"Not one that was strong enough to rupture the hull or the sail, and we're getting approximately the same radiation level from all sides, which means — I don't know what it means," Borodine admitted.

"Neither do I."

Borodine pointed to the monitor where the RAD was clearly visible, and said, "She's going to come back on board hot."

"How much more running time does it have?" Boxer asked.

"About three minutes more than the time it will take to recover ... give or take ten seconds."

"If we leave her, she'll go down to —"

"The bottom. Just a dozen feet from the boat is four thousand feet," Borodine said.

Boxer rubbed his chin... He'd have preferred to let the sea wash the contamination from the RAD, but the device was too valuable to lose. He might have to use it again... "As soon as she's aboard, begin decontamination. She's got to be brought down to a safe level."

"We could capture her and keep her outside, until we got acceptable dosimeter readings," Borodine suggested.

"We'd have to put men outside."

"At least one team to secure her."

Boxer rubbed his chin again... It would be much easier to decontaminate the special diving suits (that were made of a leadpolymer) than decontaminate the RAD... "Do it," Boxer said. Then he added, "We're going to have to send men aboard the boat, if we are really going to find out what happened."

"I was thinking exactly the same thing," Borodine said.

"Let's go by the numbers," Boxer said. "We'll secure the RAD first, then we'll deal with the other matter."

Borodine nodded and said, "I'll lead the team that goes aboard the boat."

"She's your boat," Boxer responded.

CHAPTER 5

Borodine and his team of six men entered the downed submarine through its escape hatch. The moment they were inside, their dosimeters emitted a shrill warning signal.

"We will have to move very fast," Borodine told the men, speaking to them by radio over a closed network. "We don't want to take any unnecessary risks." Then, actuating another switch, he said, "Alpha team inside escape chamber, opening hatch to CR."

"Roger that," Boxer answered.

Borodine undogged the hatch and pulled it open. "CR fully illuminated," he reported. Suddenly his heart began to race, and as he dropped to the deck, he saw several of the men. All of them were at or near their stations, and all of them were dead, including his old friend, the boat's skipper. The CR suddenly became as quiet as a tomb. As a sudden shiver shook him, he remembered the ancient tombs he had seen years before, when he'd visited Egypt.

He swallowed hard. Dividing his half-dozen men into three teams of two, Borodine sent them to investigate the various sections of the boat, while he went directly into the captain's quarters.

In minutes, each team reported finding the members of the boat's various divisions dead.

Borodine radioed the information to Boxer, who in turn asked, "Is there any evidence of reactor system failure?"

"Negative," Borodine answered. "I am returning with the log, and whatever else I think may give us some clue to what happened."

"Can you bring back one of the bodies?" Boxer asked. "Dr. Ioff might be able to determine the cause of death."

"Roger that," Borodine replied.

"Did the mayday come off a continuous tape?" Boxer questioned.

"Yes... The tape is here, in the captain's cabin," Borodine said.

"Can you shut down the reactor system?"

"Yes... I will do that just before I leave."

"You don't have much time... Ten minutes at the most, before your suits begin to fail."

"Roger that," Borodine answered, as he put the boat's log and other papers he'd gathered into a waterproof pouch.

Boxer paced the width of the CR, and at the same time watched the TV monitors... The six men would have to spend hours in the decontamination chamber, before they could be allowed back into the operating space of the SSN-S1.

"Sir, weather conditions topside are worsening," the young lieutenant reported.

Boxer acknowledged the information with a quick nod.

"Reactor down," Borodine radioed. "Moving toward escape hatch."

Boxer answered with, "Standing by."

"Moving body from CR," Borodine said.

"Any problem with that?"

"Negative," Borodine answered.

The body chosen was that of a short, wiry man; he was carried by two of the men. As soon as they entered the escape hatch area, a line was placed under his arms so that he could be towed back to the SSN-S1.

"Escape hatch flooding," Borodine reported.

"Roger that," Boxer answered.

Two minutes later Borodine and his men were out of the stricken boat, and on their way back to the SSN-S1.

Suddenly, the distinctive high-pitched chirping of killer whales filled the CR.

"Where the hell are they?" Boxer asked, looking up at the UWIS, which only showed the downed boat and Borodine's team.

"Below us," the SO answered, "and closing fast."

Boxer bit his lower lip... Killer whales could move at forty knots... He changed the UWIS's operational mode, saw that there was a pod of six adult killer whales, moving toward the boat. This species of dolphin was not only the most efficient killer, but it was also the most intelligent creature in the sea, and one of the most curious...

Abruptly, the leader, a huge bull, stopped moving in a straight line, and began to go in a circle. "He's getting their scent," another officer commented.

"Igor, there are killer whales below us... The bull is trying to locate you," Boxer radioed.

"Roger that," Borodine answered calmly.

"We'll try to divert them," Boxer said.

"Close with us."

"Roger that," Boxer responded, and immediately dialed in SLOW AHEAD.

The SSN-S1 gave a slight shudder, and began to move.

"All high-power lights on," Boxer said.

"High-power lights on," reported the WO.

Boxer looked at the UWIS display. The killer whales were still moving toward Borodine.

"Sir, Dr. Ioff requests permission to enter the CR," a junior officer said.

Boxer glanced toward the open bulkhead door. She was looking straight at him. He nodded and said, "Permission granted."

"I heard the men were returning," she said, coming alongside of him.

He nodded, pointed to the UWIS, and said, "They might not let that happen."

"What are they?" she questioned, her voice almost a whisper.

"Killer whales."

"I —" She swallowed hard. Her brow was suddenly beaded with perspiration.

"Alpha leader, you might have to use your stun prods," Boxer radioed.

"Roger that," Borodine answered. "How big are they?"

"All mature."

"That doesn't give us much leeway," Borodine answered. "Each rod has enough juice for two jolts on something that big."

"Cut the body loose if you have to," Boxer said.

"Roger that," Borodine answered.

"Those orcas have increased their speed," the SO reported.

Boxer was already aware of that. They were moving in a tight formation at thirty-five knots. "Alpha team, listen up," Boxer said. "I'm going to let those whales get close to you, then I'm going to come on at flank to hit their formation broadside. I'm going to aim for the leader."

"Roger that," Borodine answered.

Ilia put her hand on his arm. "Do you think it will work?" she asked.

"It seems to be the only game in town," Boxer answered, aware of the lightness of her touch.

She gave him a quizzical look.

"It's the only idea I have," Boxer answered, slowing the SSN-S1 to less than one third ahead and more than slow ahead.

The killer whales moved well ahead of the boat.

Ordering a change of course, Boxer positioned the boat at a ninety-degree angle to the pod of killer whales. Then visually targeting the bull leader, he called out, "Flank speed."

"Flank speed," the WO called out, as he repositioned the boat's speed control on the Master Control Console.

Within moments, the SSN-S1 responded and was making fifty knots.

"Looking good," Boxer said, viewing the UWIS.

"Closing fast," the SO reported. "Four thousand yards."

Boxer nodded.

"Are you really going to crash into the whale?" Ilia asked. She no longer had her hand on his arm, but was standing very close to him.

"Only if he wants me to," Boxer answered.

Suddenly, the boat jounced, throwing Ilia against Boxer, who caught her, and instantly let go of her.

"The same thing has happened."

He nodded, and taking hold of the 1MC mike, he switched it on. "All hands, now hear this… All hands, now hear this… The klaxon is going to sound several times. Remain at your present stations." Boxer switched off the 1MC, and pressed the klaxon button three times.

The orcas veered away, then suddenly changed their course, and headed straight for the SSN-S1.

"That bull won't be happy —"

Another jounce rocked the boat.

A red light began to flash on the SDB.

The phone connecting the CR with EO rang. Boxer answered it.

"Sir, according to the computer simulation, we have three minutes before the drive shaft begins to crack," the EO said.

"Two and a half minutes from now, reduce speed to one third ahead," Boxer told him.

"Aye, aye, sir," the EO answered.

The pod of killer whales was a hundred yards in front of them.

"That bull is going to be splattered," Boxer said, now aware that Ilia had braced herself against him by lacing her hands on his right shoulder.

Boxer sucked in his breath and waited for the killer whale to commit suicide, but at the last moment, the orca swung off to the port side. The rest of the pod followed.

"They're gone!" she exclaimed in a whisper.

"Gone," Boxer repeated, emitting a loud sigh of relief.

Ilia jerked herself away from him, and with her face suddenly coloring, she said, "Excuse me, Admiral. I had no idea —"

"No need to apologize, doctor," Boxer said. With a smile, he added, "The pleasure was mine, and I hope yours, too."

Her color became more pronounced.

He was about to suggest that they go to the wardroom for coffee, while Borodine and his team were being recovered, but the phone from engineering rang again.

"Sir, the shaft has developed several hairline cracks," the EO reported.

"Give me the bottom line," Boxer said, more tersely than he'd intended to.

"Eight knots... And I would recommend staying on the surface or traveling at periscope depth, so that we could blow ballast and break water quickly, should another emergency arise."

Boxer thanked him. Putting the phone down, he looked over at the WO. "Six knots, ahead."

"Six knots, ahead," the WO responded. Then looking at Ilia, Boxer told her what the problem was.

She nodded.

"I have traveled on the surface of this ocean during the winter," he said grimly.

"But why can't we stay at periscope depth, if that is an option?" she asked.

"Because, if something else *does* go wrong, being at sixty feet would be as dangerous as being at six hundred."

"Alpha team on UWIS," an officer reported.

"Take them aboard," Boxer responded, then to Ilia he said, "It will be at least five hours before they're out of decontam."

She nodded.

"Would you join me for coffee?" Boxer asked.

"Yes."

Again, Boxer turned his attention to the WO. "As soon as Alpha team is safely aboard, let me know... I'll either be in the wardroom or in my cabin."

"Aye, aye, sir," the WO replied.

"Suddenly, I am ravenously hungry," Boxer said to Ilia, as they left the CR.

"I am, too," she said in a low, throaty voice.

It took Boxer a moment to realize the other meaning behind her words, and as he looked at her, he found her looking up at him. Her lips were slightly parted, her blue eyes were full of flashing light, and even under the coveralls she wore, he could see the rise and fall of her breasts in time to her rapid breathing.

He stopped, and with his right hand, brushed the tips of his fingers across her cheek. "Coffee," he said softly.

Quickly, she took hold of his hand, pressed her lips against its palm, and echoed, "Coffee."

Boxer sat across from Ilia at a table in the wardroom. For several minutes neither of them had said a word. Then Ilia broke the silence by apologizing. "It was a stupid thing to do," she said, keeping her eyes lowered.

"Not as stupid as some of the things I have done in my life," Boxer answered.

She looked up at him. "It won't happen again."

Boxer nodded... He wasn't going to ask her what had caused her sudden emotional retreat. He understood, probably better than she, how particular situations can ignite them.

"I don't want an entanglement," Ilia said. "Especially one that starts in circumstances like this."

He'd misjudged her: she was more savvy than he'd thought she was. "Yes, you're right," he said. "This place, this time, hasn't any relationship to what is normal."

"I —"

The phone rang.

Boxer excused himself and answered it.

"Sir, Alpha team has been recovered," the XO reported.

Boxer thanked him, and clicking off, dialed the decontamination room.

Borodine ID'd himself.

"Damn good job," Boxer told him. Even as he spoke, the klaxon signaled that they were surfacing.

Borodine chuckled and said, "Thanks for not allowing us to be fish bait."

"You'd have done the same for me," Boxer answered.

"Yes, I would have."

"We have another slight problem," Boxer said, and before Borodine could ask what it was, he told him about the hairline cracks in the drive shaft.

"Is that why we're surfacing?" Borodine asked.

"We'll be on the surface all the way back to Norfolk," Boxer said.

"It's going to be a frozen hell up there this time of year," Borodine commented.

"I've been through it a couple of times," Boxer answered.

"Yes, I know, and so have I," Borodine said.

"I'll see you in a few hours," Boxer told him.

"I guess there's no way to avoid that," Borodine laughed.

"None," Boxer said, also laughing. He put the phone back in its cradle and returned to the table.

Borodine sat in his cabin and began to read the downed boat's log, starting with the last entry, which indicated that the entire crew was too sick to carry on their duties. According to the captain, the illness came on suddenly, after they had found and reconnoitered a nuclear hot zone, at 60 n. lat, 180 e. long...

Borodine immediately brought this information to Boxer, who fixed the position in the Bering Sea Basin, south of St. Matthew Island.

"Someone must be dumping nuclear waste there," Boxer said.

Borodine agreed.

"My guess is that there's a huge crevasse, or just a very deep undersea hole."

"There's nothing in the log that indicates that," Borodine said.

"It seems as if we've stumbled on a problem, Igor... A problem that some people might not want anyone to know about."

"The question is whether we take care of it now, or whether we —"

Borodine shook his head. "We're in no condition to do anything, Jack."

Boxer thought for a moment, then he said, "You're right... We're exhausted, and so are the men... We'll head home."

CHAPTER 6

When Negron arrived at the officer's club, he took his time going into the restaurant. He saw several officers he knew, and stopped to chat with two. The first was Lieutenant Firgison — originally from Kansas — who worked in the Bureau of Personnel; the second was Commander Daniel Holmes, assigned to the Sea Safety Research Unit, but whose real assignment, like his own, was with the Office of Naval Intelligence.

Holmes came from New York, and despite his years in the Navy, still spoke with a definite New York accent.

"How have you found the weather?" Holmes questioned, which was his way of asking if the investigation was making progress.

"Better than expected," Negron answered.

"Drink?" Holmes offered.

"Another time."

The two men nodded at each other, and Negron continued into the club's main room, where he found Hale seated in a booth next to a tanned, raven-haired woman, wearing a plunging V-neck burnt orange cocktail dress.

"Lillian, Commander Negron," Hale said, introducing them.

Negron bent slightly forward to shake her hand, and got an eyeful of her breasts.

Hale gestured to the empty bench opposite him. "What are you drinking?" he asked.

"Glenlivet neat," Negron answered.

Hale got the attention of the waiter. "Two of the same here, and one Glenlivet straight... And bring us some munchies, will you?" he asked, handing the man a folded bill.

"Certainly, sir," the waiter said, and hurried away.

"I can tell you," Hale said, "that there wasn't anything like this for the enlisted men... Nothing. Still isn't."

Negron couldn't keep his eyes off Lillian. She was a strikingly beautiful woman.

"Well, sailor man, what's the good word?" Hale asked, draping his left arm around Lillian's shoulders, and moving his fingers over the exposed top of her left breast.

"The weather has worsened," Negron answered.

"I already know that... Tell me something I don't know."

Negron's eyes darted to Lillian.

"Go for a walk," Hale ordered.

"Where?" she asked.

"How do I know *where*? Anywhere. Come back in fifteen minutes."

She pouted, but she left the table.

"Now, tell me something I don't know," Hale said.

"They've surfaced."

"What the hell does that mean?" Hale asked.

Negron shrugged.

"Christ, what *do* you know?" Hale growled.

"It would not be SOP."

"That tells me a lot."

"If they're not using standard procedure, then something has made them change."

"*Something* doesn't mean anything," Hale said. "I have to know —"

The waiter returned to the table with their drinks.

Hale waited until he was gone before continuing. "I need to know what they know."

"That's going to come under top secret classification… Perhaps, even higher."

Hale took several deep drags on his cigar, making the tip flare red… "I don't give a flying fuck if the information is marked *for the President's eyes only*. I want it!"

"It's going to cost."

"You get it and I'll pay," Hale said, "And just to sweeten the pot, I'll let you play with Lillian, and I know you'd like that."

"Yes, I'd like that," Negron answered.

Hale leered at him. "Yeah, all the men who meet her would like that. But that's a very special perk. Know what I mean?"

"I know what you mean," Negron said.

Boxer stood on the topside bridge. Because of the damaged drive shaft, the SSN-S1 had to be operated as if it was a surface craft. But even a ship designed to operate in the Arctic would have had difficulties in a Force 9 gale, let alone a twenty-five-thousand-ton, cigar-shaped boat.

"This is going to go to a Force 10," Sarkis said, steadying himself against the roll of the boat.

"We'll rotate the bridge detail every hour," Boxer said. "That goes for the WO. I want every officer to take his turn up here."

"Yes, sir," Sarkis answered.

"Even if it means a change of course, stay with the open water channels. This boat wasn't built to ram ice."

Boxer opened the hatch, dropped through it, and immediately pulled it shut after himself. There wasn't much warmth inside, but at least there wasn't any wind, and that made a considerable difference.

He dropped through another hatch, into the CR, where he removed his arctic outerwear. The warmth of the CR felt good.

Borodine was in the captain's chair, and when he saw Boxer, he said, "Are you warm enough to listen to some very bad news?"

"When I saw you, I knew I wasn't going to hear anything good," Boxer answered, with a straight face.

"Your place or mine?" Igor asked.

"Mine, naturally."

Borodine nodded and left the captain's chair.

"What I like about you," Boxer said, as they left the CR together, "is that you don't have to be coaxed; you're easy."

"The boat's log is still contaminated... But we can read it, using a mirror," Borodine explained, as they headed for the wardroom. This area had become their unofficial office, because it was where the coffee urn was located.

"How is it being neutralized?"

"Liquid nitrogen is being used as the decontaminant; then the gas is leaked."

Boxer nodded and helped himself to a mug of steaming coffee. "You wouldn't believe that I'm still cold, and I was only on the bridge for ten minutes."

"I'd believe it," Borodine answered, filling a mug with hot coffee for himself.

The two of them sat down at a table.

"I read the log's last eight pages, starting with the last entry," Borodine explained. "The skipper described his own, as well as the crew's symptoms. Every man aboard the boat died from acute radiation sickness."

"Does the Comrade Doctor's autopsy confirm that?"

"It will, when she's done."

"All of them died from fulminating multiple myeloma," Borodine said with conviction. "I have seen it before. Not only in the people who were in or very close to Chernobyl, but some who were aboard our nuclear boats when accidents occurred."

Boxer had heard of multiple myeloma, but never with the word fulminating used to describe it. He sipped the hot black coffee, then setting the mug on the table, he said, "All right, that could have meant —"

"This time it didn't happen because of an internal failure... The log clearly shows that the boat had found a hot zone in the North Pacific, a place that someone is using to dispose of nuclear waste."

"Was that just a supposition?"

Borodine shook his head. "All the instrument readings bear it out."

"Its position —"

"Latitude and longitude down to the second," Borodine said.

As was often his habit when he was thinking, Boxer ran his hand over his chin several times. Then he said, "This boat is going to have a problem making it out of here, let alone backtracking and leaving the Arctic by way of the Bering Sea."

"I know that," Borodine replied.

"Tell me more about the log entries," Boxer said.

"The hot zone is in a small canyon."

"Was there any indication of size?"

"Roughly a half mile long, a quarter of a mile wide, and — get ready for this — according to the fathometer, four miles deep."

Boxer gave a long, low whistle.

"Here's another fact worthy of the same kind of reaction," Borodine said. "The bottom temperature went off the red mark… On our instrumentation that's one thousand centigrade."

Boxer gave another long, low whistle.

"Given sufficient heat — Well, in that part of the world, along the Pacific rim of fire, a large underwater nuclear explosion might have catastrophic consequences."

Boxer agreed, and said, "I think we've stumbled on to something that we shouldn't have."

"That's my feeling, too," Borodine replied, and then added, "The real question is what are we going to do with the information that we have."

"Nothing, now. We will not give any indication to either my people or yours that we found anything unusual until we're back in the States… I don't want to risk having anyone come after us, when we're in no position to either defend ourselves, or run."

"Off the top of your head, have you any ideas about who's doing the dumping?" Borodine asked.

"None… Do you?"

Borodine shook his head. "But whoever it is, he has to have very strong government connections to your government as well as mine, or we wouldn't have been told to ignore the mayday signal by both our governments."

Boxer finished drinking the last bit of coffee in the mug, before he said, "Maybe by the time we're back in Norfolk, we will have come up with something more."

"Maybe."

"Not until we're out of the Arctic. That has to be our number one problem."

"Are you going to break radio silence and inform your people that we're running on the surface?"

"They already know that from SOSUS, and they also know we're running at greatly reduced speed, and if there's one smart operator there, he should be able to tell that our shaft is damaged."

Smiling impishly, Borodine said, "Imagine if they had *all* the information to go on."

"Yeah, they might really know what they're doing," Boxer answered.

Suddenly, the dull booming sound of two explosions penetrated the boat's hull. Moments later a louder explosion followed.

Even before Boxer left the table to get to the phone, it rang.

Sarkis ID'd himself. "The SO reports that two ash cans were dropped on the Russian boat, and destroyed it."

"Roger that," Boxer responded. Putting down the phone, he said, "Your people just destroyed the boat."

Borodine shook his head.

"That's one way of getting rid of evidence," Boxer said, returning to the table. "And one way of telling us that somehow some of your people and some of mine are involved in something that they want to hide."

"*Hide* doesn't even begin to describe what they want to do; they want to bury it."

"They might try to bury us, too," Boxer said.

"I was thinking exactly the same thing."

Boxer shrugged. "Right now our problem is to get this boat and its crew safely back to home port... I don't want to be caught here during the winter."

"If that happens —"

"We have to make sure that it won't happen," Boxer said resolutely. "When we get down to a lower latitude, there's still the possibility that some of Fong Shun Un's people will be waiting for us. Over the last few days, it's been hard to remember that we are carrying a fortune in gold."

Borodine chuckled. "I don't think too many of the crew have had any difficulty remembering."

"Like visions of fairies and sugar plums in the heads of children on Christmas Eve, I'm sure our men have dreamt about the gold."

They started to walk out of the wardroom. "Haven't *you* thought about the gold — your share of it, I mean?"

"Not in any concentrated way... I already have more money than I can use in a lifetime... I haven't thought much about it at all... What about you?"

"I have... There are things that I'd like to have... A home of my own... Perhaps a summer home as well. Other material things that I can not afford on the money I earn. And money for my son's university education."

Boxer smiled. "That and much more has already been provided."

Stopping suddenly, Borodine exclaimed, "You're joking!"

Boxer put his hand on his friend's shoulder, and said, "How was I to know that you were going to become a millionaire on your own?"

The two of them looked at one another; then simultaneously exploded into guffaws.

"You are, as the man says, 'something else,'" Borodine said, slapping Boxer on the back. "You really are something else!"

CHAPTER 7

It was 2:30 A.M. when Negron, wearing civies, entered the lobby of the luxury co-op just off Rock Canyon Drive, and told the uniformed man at the security desk, "I'm here to see Ms. Lillian Forbes."

"She expecting you?"

Negron wasn't in the mood for question and answer games. He'd gone through a great deal of trouble to track her down, and had waited for her to drive her white Trans Am into the building's subterranean garage.

"This make a difference?" he asked, flashing a NIO ID. "It better, or you're in deep shit."

"Yeah, it makes a difference... Who should I say —"

"Say nothing... Just give me the key to her apartment."

"I can't do —"

Negron nodded. "You can, and you will, or I'll find some reason for the local cops to harass the hell out of you."

"Twenty-eight-oh-two," the man said, handing him a key from a rack below the counter top.

Negron nodded, and said, "And don't announce me, understand?"

"Yeah, I understand."

Hale answered the phone.

"She has a visitor," the man on the other end said.

"Who?"

"No name... He flashed a Fed ID."

"A Fed ID?"

"Yeah... Had his picture on it."

Hale propped himself up on his elbows. He'd had her apartment wired before she moved in. Every time she had a guest, he knew what she said and what her guest said. It was just a precaution, and now and then tapes were fun to listen to, and to play for some of his friends. Lately, he had been thinking of installing hidden camcorders in the bedroom and bathroom. "What's the guy look like?"

"Got his picture on the videotape," the man said. "You want to come over and look at it?"

"Nah, as long as you have his picture, it can wait," Hale said.

"You're the boss."

"Thanks for calling," Hale said. "I'll send someone over for the tape in the morning."

"It'll be ready," the man said.

Hale put the phone down, and easing himself into a comfortable position, he wondered if Lillian had decided to do some freelancing?... If she had, he'd have to put a stop to it, or get rid of her... Moments later, he closed his eyes and slept.

Negron walked through the open elevator door, turned around, and pressed the button marked 28. The door closed, and the elevator started up... The reason for the visit was as much business as it was personal. He wanted to find out how much Lillian knew about Hale's activities, and besides, the moment he saw her, he was attracted to her. And that was something that hadn't happened too often since his divorce from Jo Ann almost two years ago...

The elevator stopped, the doors opened, and Negron stepped out into the green carpeted hallway. Lillian's apartment was off to the right, at the end of the hallway. There were only six apartments on the floor.

He inserted the key in the lock, turned it, slowly opened the door, stepped inside the large foyer, and eased the door shut. For several moments, he remained where he was. The apartment, from what he could see, was a penthouse. There was a sliding glass door that lead from the living room, directly in front of him, to a terrace. To his right, a light was on in what he guessed was a bedroom, and he was sure he heard the sound of running water coming from a bathroom, which was probably off the bedroom.

With his heart suddenly going like a trip-hammer, Negron went toward the bedroom... What he was doing went beyond a dedication to duty. He was breaking the regulations he had lived by for his entire adult life, and the civilian laws he'd sworn to uphold...

He was inside the bedroom, and he'd guessed right about the bathroom: it was off the bedroom. Now all he had to do was wait until she finished showering.

Negron took several deep breaths. The trip-hammer beating of his heart slowed to a more normal rhythm. He began to be aware of his surroundings. Everything in the room from the bed to the chaise lounge was French Provincial, and there was a subtle floral scent in the room. He found himself wondering whether he was looking at Lillian's taste, or was it the taste of a very expensive interior decorator?

He pursed his lips. The old anger flared... One of the worst arguments he and Jo Ann had had was about whether or not to hire an interior decorator. She wanted to. He didn't, claiming that he wanted their house to reflect their taste, not some third party's. He hadn't known then that she was sleeping with that third party. He found that out when he came home early two days later, and walked in on them...

Suddenly, he realized that the sound of the shower had stopped, and was replaced with the sounds of movement. His heart began to race again, and rivulets of sweat skidded down his back.

Illegal entry, he silently told himself... There was still time to get out... Then, there wasn't. Stark naked she stood in the doorway between the bathroom and the bedroom. From the rapid rise and fall of her bare breasts, he could tell that her heart was beating fast, too.

He wanted to apologize for being there, but before he could find the words and say them, she moved out of the doorway, and went toward the bed.

Suddenly, it registered. She was going to the night table drawer.

He reached behind himself, under his jacket, and pulled out a snub nose .38. "Freeze!" he barked.

She stopped.

"Put something on," he said.

She looked at him questioningly.

"Go ahead and put something on."

She went to the closet, took out a white silk robe, and slipped it on.

He waved the gun toward the bed. "All right, sit down."

She obeyed.

Negron went to the night table, opened the drawer, and picked up a nickel-plated .22 automatic. He removed the clip, and jumped the round out of the chamber; then putting the .22 back in the open drawer, and closing it, he said, "That's not a toy."

"If it was, I wouldn't have it," she snapped back.

Negron moved away from the night table, and looked at her. She was beautiful.

She looked straight back at him.

"All right, it's time to talk," he said, replacing the snub in its holster.

"Is that what you call it?" she questioned. "Talk, not rape."

"Rape?"

"Isn't that why you came here?"

"You think —" He shook his head. "You — You're not joking, are you?"

"What would you think, if you were me?" she asked, shifting her position.

"I wouldn't think that," Negron said defensively. "I wouldn't immediately jump to the worst possibility."

"I didn't jump to the worst... The worst would have been that you'd rape, then kill me."

He shook his head again. "I came here to talk... I need to know everything about Hale that you know."

She gave him a quizzical look.

"Are you his mistress?" Negron asked. The question was out of his mouth before he could stop it.

"We have an arrangement."

"Sex for money, for these digs!" he exclaimed with obvious disgust.

"And what do you do for him, Commander, to earn your keep?" she challenged.

He flushed.

"I'm a working girl... Translated, that means I'm a high-priced call girl... Any more questions?"

"Not about that," Negron answered. Her candor about herself caught him off guard, and he found himself becoming angry, though he wasn't sure why.

"The ball is in your court," she said. "Oh, I forgot, you want to know everything I know about Hale, but we somehow got sidetracked, didn't we?"

She was being sarcastic, and she had a right to be. After all, he was the one who had invaded her privacy. Not the other way around.

"Let's begin with his friends," Negron said. "You must know some of them."

She smiled up at him.

"All right, you do," he said sharply.

"What do you want to know?" she asked, with a hint of a smile still playing on her full lips.

"Who they are. What they do. What Hale really does."

"The last one is easy: Hale makes money."

"That I already guessed," Negron commented.

"He has a couple of Russian friends… People who are with the Russian Embassy, here in Washington."

"Names."

She shook her head.

He was going to insist that she must know some of Hale's Russian friends by name, when she said, "They are whoever they want to be. Just as I am. That way there's no chance for a slip up at some future date."

"What about the KGB?" he asked.

"What about them?" She shrugged.

"They're always there — unless?"

"Unless what?"

Negron didn't want to call them her *dates*, but couldn't think of any other word to describe them.

"Unless what?" she repeated.

"Unless your *dates* were KGB, or the KGB permitted them," he said. Then, after a momentary pause, he added, "The former is the more probable answer."

"So, what does it mean?" Lillian questioned.

"Hale is into something that he shouldn't be."

"There's nothing new in that... He has often said 'the only way to make real money is to bypass all the rules and regulations, especially the regulations.'"

"Yeah, that sounds like him... What about his other friends?"

"Most of them have something to do with nuclear power," she answered.

"How do you know that?"

"The guys I —"

"All I want to know is *how* you know," he said. "Nothing more."

"Why does it bug you when I tell you —"

"It doesn't."

"Listen, you came up here. I didn't go to you," she said, suddenly standing up. "I saw the look you gave me, when we met at the table."

"I don't know what you're talking about."

"Not much you don't..." She was pacing back and forth now, across the length of the room. "You came for information... Well, I told you what I know."

"Calm down," he said.

"Listen, Commander, I'm not in the Navy... You can't give me orders."

"I'm not giving you an order. I'm asking you to please calm down."

"I'm calm," she said, stopping. "I'm cool. But I could use a drink."

"So could I."

She headed for the kitchen, and he followed her. It had been years since he'd been anywhere near a prostitute, or as she called herself, *a working girl.* When he was younger, before he married, he'd had several episodes with call girls. But they didn't leave any sort of an impression…

Lillian opened the refrigerator. "You can have ginger ale, diet Coke, Perrier, or beer."

"Perrier would be fine."

She took out the liter bottle, poured two tall glasses, replaced the bottle, and closed the door. "I'd offer you something to eat," she said, handing him one of the two glasses, "but all I have are munchies, and they will really make you thirsty."

"We could order up a pizza," he said with a smile. He suddenly realized that when he'd finally leave, he'd go back to his small apartment near the Navy Yard and be alone. And now looking at her, with the glass in her hand, and her long blonde hair flowing down to her shoulders, and her green eyes locked with his, he didn't want to be alone. He wanted to be with her. "It was just an idea," he said, aware of the silence between them.

"Another time, maybe," she told him.

He nodded, thanked her for the drink, and after he put the empty glass down on the kitchen counter, he started to walk out of the room.

She followed him. "Now, there's one thing *I'd* like to know," she said.

"And what's that?"

They'd reached the apartment's door. He turned and faced her.

"Whose side are you really on?" she asked, looking up at him.

Negron smiled. She almost looked like an innocent young woman.

"Why the smile?"

Negron told her.

She cast her eyes down. "You're making fun of me."

"No," he said quietly. "I am not making fun of you... Perhaps, I am making fun of myself."

She looked up at him again. "Really, whose side are you on?"

"I'll let you answer that."

"But —"

Suddenly, Negron reached out, put his arms around her, and drawing her to him, kissed her lips. He felt her arms circle him, then her fingers on the back of his neck. Separating from her, he told her, "I wanted to do that from the moment I saw you."

"Dressed or undressed?"

"Now who's making fun of whom?"

"I'm not making fun of you," she said, gently moving out of his embrace. "I wanted you to kiss me..."

He tried to take her in his arms again.

She stepped back. "I want us to have our own time, our own date."

Suddenly, he understood: she'd either been with Hale, or with one of his friends... Perhaps with both men?

"Don't be angry," she said softly.

"I'm not," Negron answered, but he was.

She put her hand his arm. "Can you get away for the weekend?"

"Yes."

"I have a small house on Emerald Island," she said. "It's just a few hundred yards from the beach, and I have a small day sailer, a cat boat."

He took hold of her hand, kissed the back of it, and said, "I accept." Then he drew her close and kissed her passionately on the lips. Moments later, he let go of her, opened the door, and left the apartment.

Negron rode the elevator down, and watched the numbers of the floors flash by. When he reached the ground floor, and the door opened, he saw two men at the desk: one was the same man he had spoken to, the other was new. Both were wearing similar uniform.

Negron glanced up at the space above the door, and saw the TV camera. He pursed his lips; he had forgotten about it. There were probably two or three cameras in the lobby... Well, better safe than sorry... He reached around to his .38, and by the time he was at the desk, he was pointing it at the two men. "Shut the security system down," he said. "Don't do anything else."

The new man reached under the counter, flicked several switches. "It's down," he said.

"Now give me the tapes."

"What!" the other man exclaimed.

"The tapes now!" Negron said, pointing the .38 straight at him.

The man hesitated.

"Give him the fuckin' tapes," the new man said.

"But —"

"They ain't worth dyin' for, Tommy," the man told him. "An' this guy looks like he knows how to use that gun."

"Believe it!" Negron said.

Tommy opened up the three tape magazines and handed Negron the three cassettes.

Negron put the cassettes down on the desk counter, reached over, and tore out the phone line. Picking up the three cassettes, he left the lobby, and quickly crossed the street to his car.

Hale picked up the phone again, recognized Tommy's voice, and said, "What the hell is going on?"

"He just took the fuckin' TV tapes."

"What?"

"He pointed a gun —"

"What the hell is going on?" Hale shouted. "I want to know what the hell is going on?"

"This guy —"

"You bring her here."

"Now?"

"Yeah, now. Bring her here," Hale shouted, and slammed the phone down... Something a lot more important was happening than her going freelance. Something a lot more important... He got out of bed, put on a blue silk bathrobe, and went into the bathroom to wash his face with cold water. He wanted to be a hundred-and-ten-percent awake when he questioned her.

CHAPTER 8

Boxer pushed open the hatch, and pulled himself up onto the bridge. Even before he was fully out of the hatch opening, a wind-driven snow lashed his face. The storm that had been brewing for several hours slammed the SSN-S1 with winds of ninety to one hundred miles an hour, causing the boat to violently pitch, roll, and yaw. With each plunge, waves broke over the forward deck, crashed into the sail, and sent a shower of spray over the men which quickly froze.

"I have the conn," Boxer shouted, above the scream of the wind.

Sarkis nodded, saluted, pulled the cover closed after himself, and disappeared into the open hatch.

Boxer checked the phone contact with Borodine in the CR. Then he said, "Switch all operations except steering to the CR. Can't see anything up here. Not even the compass."

"Wouldn't do you much good in these latitudes, even if you could," Borodine answered.

Boxer agreed and switched off. Though he'd only been on the bridge for five minutes, the freezing temperature, made colder by the wind chill factor, gave him the feeling that the cold was inside him.

He glanced over at the starboard side lookout. That man and the port side lookout were on a raised platform directly behind the control portion on the bridge. Both men were fully exposed to the fury of the wind and the snow.

Boxer shook his head and faced front again. It would be days before they were out of the Arctic, and an even longer time before they would reach the East Coast, where the weather and the water would be calmer.

The red phone light blinked.

Boxer picked it up. "Bridge," he said.

"The RO reports pressure ridges ten miles ahead, extending thirty miles to the north, and fifty miles to the south."

"Can we get a satellite pic of them?" Boxer asked.

"Already in the works," Borodine answered. "The next pass over will be in thirty minutes."

"Roger that," Boxer said. Replacing the phone, he flailed his arms several times to break the coating of ice that had formed on them. Then he beat his chest to get the ice off of it.

The hatch opened, and the new watch reported to the DO.

The last man out of the hatch saluted Boxer and, in English grounded in Russian accent, said, "The Comrade Doctor asked me to give you this." He handed a thermos to Boxer.

Deeply touched by Ilia's gesture, Boxer exercised his limited use of Russian, and thanked him. Then he handed the thermos back to the man, and said, "Drink." And he made a circular gesture to include all of the men. "Everyone drink."

"For you," the man said, holding out the thermos to him. "Comrade Doctor —"

"For everyone on bridge," Boxer said.

The man hesitated, then said something in Russian to the other men, opened the thermos, and drank. "Tea, hot tea!"

By the time the thermos reached Boxer, there was only enough for two good swallows. But it was hot, and that was what mattered most. He stowed the thermos in a small locker under the control panel.

The minutes dragged by, and the first half hour passed.

The phone light blinked again.

Boxer answered it.

"Got several pics," Borodine said. "But none have really good definition. Even using computer enhancement, the definition isn't that good... Now for the bad news."

"You telling me that what you just told me was the good news?"

"I don't make the news, I just report it," Borodine said.

Boxer smiled. His Russian counterpart sounded more and more like an American.

"The pressure ridges extend back at least ten miles," Borodine said.

"That's not a joke," Boxer responded.

"It wasn't meant to be."

Boxer uttered a ragged sigh, and asked, "Do we have any indication of which way the ridge is moving?"

"South at two knots, from what we can make out."

"I was hoping to blast our way through it. But ten miles —!"

"We might try to flank it," Borodine suggested.

"I don't want to go any further north than we are, and as for trying to swing around it to the south ... that ice could change direction and block us."

"Then the only other alternative is to go under it," Borodine said.

"That's not much of an alternative," Boxer responded, then he added, "We'd better be damn sure about what we're going to do... Damn sure!"

"Growlers, ten degrees off port bow," the lookout reported.

"Out," Boxer said into the phone, and replaced it in its cradle.

"Big ones!" the lookout called.

Boxer already had the infrared glasses turned on the small icebergs. They were very big. Some were fifty feet across, easily as long, and at least two feet thick.

"Growlers, dead ahead," the same lookout shouted.

"Slow ahead," Boxer immediately ordered.

"Slow ahead," the second bridge officer repeated.

In minutes they were in the band of packed ice, and the floes were crashing into them.

Boxer had been in a similar situation years before, and had had his boat frozen in the ice for several days, until a sudden warming trend enabled him to break free and dive beneath the ice.

"Reduce speed to 900 rpms," Boxer said.

"Reducing speed to 900 rpms," the young officer repeated.

Because of the storm, some of the growlers crashed down on the boat's deck, broke apart, and dropped back into the sea. But others remained on the deck, and all too quickly, a weird-looking ice structure was being built up whose weight pushed the deck deeper into the water, making it easier for more ice to land on it.

Boxer called the CR. "I need four ice chopping details topside, now."

"Roger that," Borodine answered.

Within minutes, sixteen men were on the deck. Each had a safety line around his waist, secured to a U-shaped bolt on the deck, and each man smashed at the ice with a sixteen-pound sledgehammer.

The men struggled to keep their footing on the heaving deck. Several times the hammer struck the deck plate. But even as they smashed the ice, more came on board.

After fifteen minutes, Boxer ordered four new details on deck to relieve the exhausted men. A man in the second shift lost his footing, went over the side, and was badly injured by a growler that slammed him against the side of the boat, before he could be pulled to safety by the other men.

Boxer realized that the storm could last for several days, and if it did, the boat either would be too badly damaged to make the long journey home, or it would have been sunk... He switched on the 1MC. "All hands, now hear this... All hands, this is Admiral Boxer... Stand by to dive... Stand by to dive." Then he pressed the klaxon's button. "Dive!" he ordered. "Dive!"

The men on the bridge detail quickly dropped through the open hatch. Boxer waited until the bridge was cleared before he left it, pulled the hatch shut after him, and dogged it.

"Periscope depth," he called out, as soon as he entered the CR.

"Periscope depth," Borodine answered.

"The ice was too much to deal with," Boxer said, as soon he'd removed his arctic outer gear, and sat down next to Borodine, who occupied the captain's chair.

Borodine nodded. "At least we'll have less motion," he answered.

"In a little while, the pressure ridges would have forced us to dive," Boxer said.

"Passing through twenty-five feet," a WO reported.

"That ice is gone by now," Boxer said, switching on the UWIS and scanning the forward deck.

"Clear?" Borodine questioned.

"Yes, clear."

"Stand by to lower sail," Borodine announced, then he switched on the 1MC. "All hands, now hear this... All hands now hear this... Rig for underwater operation... Rig for underwater operation."

Boxer changed the boat's speed from 900 rpms, just to hold steerageway, to six knots.

"Periscope depth," the WO reported.

"Roger that," Borodine acknowledged.

"The weather topside would have devoured the men," Boxer said, suddenly realizing that he'd left the thermos in the bridge locker.

"The dive is very risky, Jack," Borodine said.

"Has the EO reported any change in the shaft?"

Borodine shook his head. "And let's all hope he doesn't. If we had to, we wouldn't be able to smash our way up through it. We'd be caught under it."

Boxer didn't answer. But he knew his friend well enough to know that he'd just been rebuked for having made the decision to dive.

Hale and Lillian were standing in the den. She'd been brought in through the door on the far side of the room, and he had come in by way of the master bedroom.

"You had a visitor," Hale said, looking at her. She wore a white blouse, a pair of blue jeans, and slip-on white sneakers.

She nodded.

"Who?" Hale asked.

"A friend."

Hale backhanded her hard across the face, knocking the girl to the floor. "Who?" he repeated.

Sobbing, she said, "Commander Negron."

He reached down, and pulled her to her feet. "I didn't know the two of you were friends, or were you doing some freelancing?"

She shook her head. "No... No... I —"

Hale balled his fist, and drove it into her right breast.

She screamed.

"What did he want?" Hale asked, and before she could answer, he said, "I got it all on tape."

"On tape?" she cried.

"Yeah, ain't that a gas… Every time you partied with one of my friends, I got it all down on tape… Makes good listening."

"Oh my God!" she wept.

"Yeah, it's a turn on for some… Tell me about the Commander… But before you do, strip."

"What?"

"Take your fuckin' clothes off," Hale ordered. "I like to look at your bare ass."

Lillian slipped her sneakers off, removed her blouse, then her jeans and briefs.

"Good… Now tell me what the Commander wanted besides your ass," Hale said, going over to the desk and taking a cigar out of the mahogany humidor.

"He had the key to the apartment," she sobbed.

"Okay, that much I know," Hale said, cutting the tip of the cigar. "Now, tell me something I don't know." He lit up, and blew several smoke rings.

"I was in the shower. I didn't know he was there. I swear!"

He came toward her. "So you come out of the shower, bare-ass naked like you are now, and then what?"

Hale shook his head, and took a deep drag on the cigar. The next instant, he grabbed her hair, twisted it in his right hand, and with his left, pushed the cigar against her right cheek.

She screamed.

"See, I'm not a patient man," Hale said, letting go of her. She dropped to the floor.

"He's… He's —"

"Tell me what he is," he roared, pushing the cigar's burning end against the top of her left breast.

She screamed again. "No… No… No… I'll tell you… I'll tell you."

"I'm listening," Hale said.

"He's ONI," she wept.

"ONI," he repeated. "The son-of-a-bitch is ONI," he shouted, pacing back and forth. "He's been stringing me along... I've been paying —" He bore down on Lillian. "What did you tell him?"

"He knew I worked for you," she wept.

"I have it on the tapes," Hale shouted, pushing his face down to hers. "But I want to hear it from you."

"I told him —"

He grabbed hold of her left breast, and squeezed it as hard as he could.

Screaming, she tried to pull away.

Lillian swallowed. "I need a tissue," she said.

"You fucking whore, tell me!" he shouted, still squeezing her breast.

"The men you sent me to," she wept.

Breathing hard, he let go of her. "The men I sent you — you gave him their names?"

She shook her head. "Only told him that some were Russian... That's all I told him."

"*That's all I told him*," he mimicked. Then he shouted, "That was too fucking much!" And slammed his fist into her face.

Blood spurted from her nose.

"I don't fuckin' need you anymore," he told her. "You're history." Then he went to the door on the other side of the room, opened it, and said, "She's yours... Tell Miguel he owes me one."

Two men came into the room; one of them held a hypodermic needle.

Lillian scrambled to her feet, and tried to run for the door.

One of the men grabbed hold of her.

Hale laughed, "Next time you wake up, you'll be in Colombia, flat on your back in some whorehouse."

Lillian screamed, bit the man on the face, under his left eye.

Cursing, he let go of her.

She ran to the window.

"Get her!" Hale shouted.

But the next instant she hurled herself through the glass. And for a few seconds, she felt the cold night air against her naked body. Then she smashed into the concrete sidewalk.

Negron held Lillian's naked body close to his own. His lips were on hers, while his hands caressed her breasts, her flat bare stomach — The ringing phone shredded his dream.

"Okay," he mumbled, and picking up the phone, he said, "Commander Negron here."

Nothing from the other end, except the sound of someone breathing.

"Hay —"

The click told him the caller wasn't on the line. He put the phone down, and looked at the digital clock on the night table. It was 5:30. The alarm was set to go off at 6:00 A.M. He had to be in the office by 7:30... Fifteen minutes less sleep wasn't going to kill him... Though he would have liked to have finished the dream. "Well, Lillian, do I call you, or don't I?" He reached for the phone, then drew his hand away. "You're too old to show how anxious you are to —"

Suddenly, gunfire blew away the door lock. The next instant, two men with black ski masks over their heads entered the bedroom firing Uzies...

Two rounds tore into Negron's chest; then the top of his head burst open, splattering his brains over the bed's backboard and the pillows.

CHAPTER 9

Even at sixty feet below the surface, the SSN-S1 responded to the violent surge of the ocean above it. From reading its various instruments, Boxer and Borodine could tell where the pressure ridges were, and where there were open areas of water. Some of these areas were large enough for the SSN-S1 to surface, but none were larger than a mile long, and at the most, a few hundred yards wide. The length and width of these openings were never stable: they lengthened and widened in response to the ferocity of the wind.

For the next fifty-six hours, Boxer and Borodine spent almost all their time in the CR, sometimes dozing in their respective chairs, and going to their cabins to shave, shower, and change their clothing. Seldom to sleep. They even had their meals brought to them. And for all of that time, neither one spoke much to the other. Their conversation was limited to the exchanges necessary to run the CR.

Only the CR watch was permitted in the Control Room. Even Stark and Ilia were banned from entering it.

It was only a short time before the other officers and men in the CR realized that there was tension between the two admirals, and that forced the men to speak in whispers, and walk, as the expression goes, as if they were walking on eggshells.

Boxer sensed the reaction of the men, and he was sure that Borodine had. But there wasn't anything he could — or for that matter *wanted* — to do about it. His decision to dive was based on his previous experiences in the Arctic and Antarctic, and though he knew that Igor had similar experiences, he had to make the decision unilaterally... Had Borodine made the decision, he would have accepted it without any sulks.

"Open water," the SO reported. "Open water, ahead from zero to eighty-nine degrees, from two hundred and seventy-five to three hundred and sixty... Range to the maximum of our system's reading, twenty-five miles."

"Roger that," Boxer said calmly, wanting very much to turn and smile at Igor.

"Surface conditions?" Borodine asked.

"Keying satellite," replied an officer.

"Last reported pictures taken forty-five minutes ago... Wind, three zero knots... Water temperature, three seven degrees... Air temperature, minus twenty degrees."

Boxer turned to Borodine. "Surface?" he asked.

"It's your decision," Borodine answered stiffly.

Boxer pursed his lips, then suddenly he said, "Admiral, in my quarters. Now!" And leaving his chair, he gave the conn to the WO. "Keep her steady as she goes."

"Aye, aye, sir," the officer answered.

Boxer hurried out of the CR, with Borodine close behind. As soon as the two of them were inside the cabin, Boxer said, "Close the door."

"The door is closed," Borodine snapped.

"I'm not going to play games," Boxer said, looking straight at his friend. "I made the call to dive, because —"

"That kind of decision should have been made jointly," Borodine answered. "And if necessary, we should have had the XO's input, and Admiral Stark's, too."

"There wasn't any time."

"There was certainly time for you to consult with me," Borodine said.

"The ice was piling up on the forward deck faster than the men could chop it away... We had one accident, and I didn't want to risk another."

"You risked everyone's life, not just having another accident. And that was something you did not have the right to do."

Boxer suddenly felt defensive. "If I —"

Borodine shook his head. "If you had informed me what the conditions were topside, I might have agreed with you... But you didn't think of doing that."

"We were down at the bow," Boxer said.

Borodine nodded. "The two of us are in command... You took it upon yourself to make an important decision without consulting either me — who should have been consulted — or anyone else."

Boxer rubbed his chin... He had never imagined that Borodine would react this way... "All right, I apologize. I had no idea that you —"

"How do you think it would have looked to your men, if *I* had given that order without first having consulted with you?" Borodine asked.

Boxer raised his eyebrows.

"My men expect me to be respected by everyone aboard, just as your men expect you to be respected."

Suddenly, Boxer realized why Borodine was as angry as he was... For him, it was not only the safety of the boat that was involved, but in the eyes of his men, his standing... "I will call the crew together, and explain. And I will apologize to you, if you think that will rectify the situation."

"This is one of the times when the differences between our cultures shows... Ours —"

"No need to explain. I will take care of it," Boxer said.

Borodine nodded, and extended his hand. "Friends?"

"More than friends, and slightly less than brothers," Boxer answered, shaking Borodine's hand.

"Then we surface?" Borodine asked.

Boxer nodded. "We surface."

For several minutes, Admiral Hays listened very carefully to the sound coming from the tape. Then he turned to the ranking officer in the Undersea Sound Analysis Laboratory, Captain Darlin, and said, "Single screw submarine. Probably one of ours."

Darlin nodded. "The SSN-S1. But now listen to this."

The technician switched on another tape.

"Sounds the same to me," Hays said, after two minutes had passed.

"Look at the two on the scope," Darlin said, as he changed the position of several switches. "The green line is the first tape... Normal sounds, though it bears the boat's individual sound signature. Now look at the second tape."

A yellow line suddenly came on to the screen.

"No difference that I can see," Hays said, but even as he spoke, very small spikes began to occur.

"Those jitters, as we call them, indicate a shaft anomaly, which caused them to surface," Darlin said. "But then we got this... This is the third tape, and it indicates that they submerged again to a depth of sixty feet." He put a third tape on the video monitor. "Notice the jitters occur with greater frequency, and not just at the two previous locations on the display line, but almost all across it."

Hays's eyes went wide. "Do you think Boxer knows?"

"Maybe... But I don't think so... The simulation equipment on board doesn't have the program to show anything more than the basic problem."

Hays moved away from the screen, and Darlin followed.

"Any idea of how long that shaft will last?" Hays asked.

"None."

"Best guess?"

"They're doing a steady six knots. That's like marching a couple of thousand men over a suspension bridge... They'd be better off changing from six to nine knots, maybe throw in a five, from time to time."

Hays nodded, thanked him, and returning the snappy salute, he left the laboratory. When he returned to his own office, he immediately contacted Communications, and ordered a Code Red message to be transmitted to the SSN-S1. Then he phoned the Chief of Naval Aviation, and ordered a plane to fly out to the SSN-S1, and drop a message, detailing the possibility of the boat's drive shaft suddenly breaking up. That done, he was about to report the latest development to Olsen, when his phone rang. Olsen was on the line.

"I was just going to phone you," Hays said.

"I have just learned from the District police that one of your men — an agent in the ONI — has been shot to death in his apartment."

Hays rested his elbows on the desk. "Name?" he asked.

"William Negron."

"Do the police have any clues?"

"They're sure it was a professional hit... A man who lives across the street saw two men, whose faces were covered with ski masks, run out of the building at about the time the murder took place."

"Not much to go on," Hays said.

"Any idea what Negron was working on?"

"None... But I will find out."

"Let me know... If you think I can help in any way, let me know."

"Thank you."

"Now, tell me why you were going to call me."

Hays explained the SSN-S1's situation. Then he said, "If that shaft breaks up, it will be like an exploding shell... Chunks of metal will fly all over the aft section of the boat. Some of them will have enough force to puncture the hull."

"Jesus Christ! Does Boxer know what his situation is?"

"Part of it... He has run submerged, after surfacing, and now is back on the surface again. My people are trying to make radio contact with him, and I have ordered a message drop, but the success of that depends on the weather."

"If that shaft goes, we lose the boat, possibly some of the crew, and the gold."

"And whatever he recovered from the Soviet boat," Hays commented.

"Yeah, that, too," Olsen answered. "Let me know what's happening."

"I will," Hays said, and he put the phone back in its cradle... He had never liked Olsen much, and, now, he liked him even less.

Detective Captain Ian Green of the NYPD Homicide Division didn't look anything like the detectives on TV. He was sixty-two, sported a gray beard, and had a bald spot on the top of his head. His brown hair was thinning, and he constantly had to fight the battle of the belly bulge. One good dinner, and he'd be up a minimum of five pounds when he weighed himself the following morning.

Green, a thirty-five-year veteran — twenty-five of which were spent in Homicide — had his specialists figure out the trajectory of the dead woman's body, and pinpointed it to a Mr. Hale's apartment on the thirty-sixth floor. Only, as he examined the premises under Hale's watchful eyes, he couldn't find any evidence of a struggle, or of broken glass.

"Are you satisfied, Captain?" Hale asked.

Green looked at Hale. He had seen his kind many times over the years. A fat cat — no, that wasn't at all fair to the cats of the world, or even to his five, all of which were well fed because Green fed them. No, Hale was just one of those wheeler-dealer types, who somehow manage to make a fortune, even though they are rotten examples of human beings. Not that Green was looking for some correlation between wealth and goodness. That would be as foolish as looking for a correlation between beauty in a woman — or handsomeness in a man — with character. He had learned a long time ago that there wasn't any.

Hale was still waiting for his answer, but Green remained silent until he was at the door, ready to leave. Then he said, "A nude woman just doesn't happen to fall out of a window, and this one, we know, flung herself out."

"But not from this apartment."

"That's not what my specialists say," Green answered directly. "They say she went out of that window behind me."

"They're wrong."

"They're never wrong," Green answered. "When we find out who she is, then we'll begin to put various things together, and one of them, Mr. Hale, will tell us why she was here, and another will tell us why she went out of the window." Then he opened the door, stepped halfway out of the apartment, stopped, faced Hale again, and said, "As the detective always says on TV, or in a film, I'll say to you: Don't leave town. And just so that you know I'm not playing games, I'll repeat it.

Don't leave town." A moment later he was out of the apartment, and on his way to the scene of another crime. A Commander William Negron had been shot to death in his apartment sometime during the early morning hours...

Hale got out of his limo at 17th and Riggs Place, and walked to French and 9th, where he waited for Miguel Pasao. In less than a minute, a white Mercedes stopped in front of him. He opened the door, and sat down next to the driver. Before he closed the door, the car was in motion.

"More fucking things happened than I want to think about," he said, aware of Miguel's lavender-scented cologne.

"So I was told," Miguel said. Then, after a pause, he asked, "Are you sure you weren't followed?"

"Miguel, what do you take me for?" Hale responded.

"Just asking."

"A fucking Detective Green went over my apartment this morning."

Miguel gave him a quick glance.

"His brain boys figured out that the body came out of one of my windows," Hale explained.

"I take it he found nothing."

"Nothing... But he's the bulldog type. He's not going to let go."

Miguel smiled. "Oh, there are all sorts of ways to make a bulldog let go."

"Yeah, I know that... But this guy might have to be put down."

Miguel nodded.

"Where are we going?" Hale asked, aware that they were heading east on New York Avenue, toward Annapolis.

"I'm thinking of buying a boat. I want to take a look at it," Miguel answered easily. "The owner wants a million two, but probably will take a million." Smiling again, he added, "I believe in combining business with pleasure."

Again there was a pause in the conversation, and the silence made Hale uncomfortable... But he was always uncomfortable around Miguel. The man was tall, thin, and muscular. He was handsome, and he knew it. And he was absolutely inscrutable. Even when he smiled, you weren't sure what prompted it, or, even more important, what it meant...

Suddenly, Hale realized that Miguel was smiling at him, as he said, "Tell me how you met Commander Negron."

"Some party at the Officer's Club," Hale answered.

"And just how did you go about recruiting him?"

"When I found out he was in OPS — that's what he told me — I thought he'd be a good source of information."

"Did you call him after the party, or did he call you?"

"I called him. But he couldn't meet me. He had a prior appointment. A few days later, he called and asked me to join him for drinks."

"And you did?"

"Yes."

"Did you run a check on him through our security system?"

"Yes... He came up clean... I was especially interested in him because of his previous submarine experience... You know about the discussions we've been having about using submarines to transport the material to the storage site?"

"Yes... I certainly can see why you were interested in him," Miguel commented, and asked to be told more.

Hale explained how Negron complained about the amount of alimony he had to pay, and that he never had enough money to do the things he wanted to. "He even said that he was thinking of leaving the Navy, and going into private business. That's when I made my move, and made an offer to him."

"And he accepted it?"

"Not right off... He said that he wanted time to think it over.

"I sweetened it by another couple of hundred a month, and he went for it the way a drowning man goes for a life preserver."

Miguel smiled.

"The information he gave me about the SSN-S1 was right on the money," Hale said. Then in a low, defensive voice, he added, "There wasn't any damn way for me to know that he was ONI."

Miguel patted Hale's knee. "I probably would have done the same thing. These days it's very hard to tell the difference between who think's he a shark and who is really a shark."

Hale felt better.

"But I am sorry about what happened to Lillian... Did she tell you why Negron visited her?"

Hale shifted his position, and before he could answer, Miguel said, "Let me put it another way... Did she tell you what she told Negron?"

"About the men I set her up with," Hale said, again in a low, defensive voice.

"And that's why you had him taken out?"

"There wasn't anything else I could have done, was there?" He looked at Miguel. But there wasn't any indication on the man's face that he had even heard the question.

As he turned the car off the main road, Miguel said, "This leads to the marina. We're only a few minutes away from it."

"Admiral Boxer and his Russian counterpart, Admiral Borodine, are our main problems," Hale said.

91

"You're probably right."

Suddenly, the car slowed, then stopped altogether.

"Goddamn fucking timing belt!" Miguel swore. "I told that shithead mechanic that it wasn't right... You stay here... I'll check under the hood." He sprung the hood open, left the car, and closed the door behind him. Moments later he was bent under the hood.

Hale moved around. He was about to open the door, when he looked up into the rear-view mirror and saw a black BMW roll to a stop some distance behind the Mercedes. He faced front, and was going to open the door, when he saw Miguel come out from under the hood, and run toward the other car.

Hale suddenly knew what was going to happen. And before he could put his hand on the door handle, there was a tremendous explosion. Fire was everywhere, even on him... He could hear himself screaming...

CHAPTER 10

Green nodded and sat down in front of Negron's boss, Admiral James Christopher. He said, "You know Admiral Commander Negron's murder is the business of the Metropolitan Police."

The Admiral, a short, thin man with closely cropped gray hair and penetrating green eyes, answered in a soft, almost caressing voice, "It's not our purpose to contest that point."

"I'm glad to hear that," Green said, aware that he was dealing with an individual who, in the vernacular, could be called a smooth son-of-a-bitch. "But I would also like to hear what your purpose is." He put special emphasis on the word *your*.

"Commander Negron was involved in a highly sensitive investigation," the Admiral said.

"Aren't we all," Green commented in a low voice.

"Pardon me?"

"I'm sorry… I said, 'Aren't we all.'"

"Aren't we all *what?*" the Admiral asked.

Green leaned slightly forward, and said, "Admiral, my time is valuable, and I'm sure yours is, too, so why don't we stop pussyfooting around and get right down to the nitty gritty." Before the Admiral could answer, Green added, "I don't want to make an issue of this, but if I have to, I will."

The Admiral flushed. "I hope that's not a threat, Captain."

"It's just a statement of fact… A man was killed on my side of the street. I want all the information you have that might give me some idea who killed him, and why."

"The why is easy... As I told you before, Commander Negron was working on a very sensitive case, and was getting very close to the heart of it."

"How close to the heart of it?"

Suddenly the Admiral's phone rang. He excused himself, picked up the phone, and said, "Admiral Christopher here." He listened for a moment. "Captain Green is right here." And he handed the phone to Green, who ID'd himself.

The voice on the other end said, "Cap'n, we got a call from the Annapolis police. They were running a routine check... Wanted to know if we got any calls for a missing person... Says some John Doe was burned alive in a late model Mercedes just inside the city line, on a back road."

"When?"

"Their best guess was sometime yesterday... They have some lab guys goin' over the car now, and the coroner, on his prelim, says the person was definitely burned alive... No signs of violence on what was left of him... Some local guy reported the fire to the fire department, and when he was questioned by the police, he said he saw a black car with a DC plate, making a U-turn, and speeding away from the burning car."

"Did he make the plate?"

"One letter and two numbers... The letter *M*, and the numbers 7 and 4."

"The best the computers can do with that is give us a couple of hundred names," Green said.

The man on the other end laughed. "Maybe a couple of thousand."

"Try it, anyway. Maybe we'll pick up a few interesting fish."

"Sure, why not."

"I'll be back shortly," Green said. Then, as he handed the phone back to the Admiral, he explained, "I'm notified whenever we get a call from the homicide sections of the police forces of various towns and cities in the area, telling us that they have an unidentified murder victim. This one was burned to death."

"I gathered someone saw the car?"

Green nodded. "And managed to get a couple letters off the plate, but not enough to help... All of it is routine. Nothing much comes of it."

"I know what you mean," the Admiral said. "Much of what we do is routine, too... Actually, Commander Negron's work was routine until just a few weeks ago."

Green said, "What changed it?"

The Admiral smiled. "I thought we were finished with that line of questioning."

"The phone call interrupted it, Admiral... I never left it."

"I'm afraid that we have come to an impasse, Captain," the Admiral said. "We will conduct our own investigation into Commander Negron's murder, and when we have all the facts, and enough information for you to arrest the murderers, then we will turn it over to you. But anything else must — for security reasons, remain with us."

Green didn't appreciate being denied information, and growling, he said, "I guess then, I'll have to get a court order... Or perhaps, I might let the press know — Yes, I think the press would have a field day with your lack of cooperation for 'security reasons.'"

"That is a threat, isn't it, Captain?"

"Well, now that you mention it, I suppose it is, Admiral. But I'm only doing my job."

The Admiral stared hard at Green, but Green locked eyes with him and never wavered.

"I will tell you this, and only this... Commander Negron mentioned a man by the name of Anthony Hale, and a woman named Lillian."

Green started out of the chair, then dropped back. "Are you sure about those names?"

The Admiral nodded. "He left a taped report at three o'clock in the morning. He was killed sometime later."

"According to the coroner, and people in the building who heard the shooting, it happened at 6:00 A.M."

"All right, I gave you all I could," the Admiral said.

Green ignored him. "Did the Commander come here to make the tape?"

"No. He used the special security phone."

"What was his connection to Hale?" Green pressed.

"Sorry, that comes under a security restriction," the Admiral said.

"What was his connection to the woman?"

"Apparently, he had just met her."

"A nude woman took a swan dive — well, not exactly a swan dive — from a window in Hale's penthouse apartment, three hours before Commander Negron was killed."

"You think it might be the woman he named?"

Green shrugged. "It's possible. If the Jane Doe turns out to be Lillian, then we have several interesting connections, don't we, Admiral?"

"Certainly more than just coincidental," Admiral Christopher answered.

Green smiled and said, "Sometimes, a little cooperation goes a long, long way, and sometimes, it even goes in two directions..."

Boxer sat drinking coffee at a table in the wardroom. Since the danger of having to run submerged under the ice pack had passed, and even the weather had sufficiently moderated to make running on the surface practical, he was again afflicted by periods of a combination of weariness and depression that, as far as he could determine, fed on each other.

Aware that someone else had entered the wardroom, he didn't look up until he heard Stark ask, "Jack, are you all right?"

"I'm all right," Boxer answered. He hadn't seen much of his old friend in recent days. Stark was wise enough not to intrude into a difficult situation.

Stark filled a mug with coffee, helped himself to a cherry Danish, and joining Boxer at the table, said, "I'm ready for another vacation." He laughed. "Maybe, I should say, I'm ready for a vacation... The last one didn't turn out to be much of a vacation. I really feel as if we're on an extension of its tail end. We still have Paskudnyak's body in the freezer."

Boxer nodded and drank some coffee from his mug, before he said, "I completely forgot... When we're south of Greenland, we'll bury Paskudnyak at sea. I think he would have wanted us to do that."

"I made a few rough calculations... His share comes to a tad under twenty million. That's what you, I, and Borodine will see, after the crew and everyone else takes their cut. No one on board will walk away with less than a million."

Boxer smiled. "Those three characters I hired on are going to be the biggest sports in town."

"The three of them are good men," Stark said. "They've changed."

"Maybe it was because they didn't have to worry about where their next meal was coming from?" Boxer offered.

"That, and the fact that they realized that they were dealing with real danger, and they were with men who dealt with it all of the time."

"Whatever caused it doesn't matter... The fact that it happened is what really counts."

"I'll drink to that," Stark said, raising the coffee mug to his lips.

"The idea of a long, restful vacation sounds real good to me," Boxer said. Then he added, "I've been toying with the idea of handing in my papers... I'm beginning to understand that there's more to life than what I have been doing over the years."

"Several million men would have gladly changed places with you," Stark said.

"Probably... But I wonder how many would have been willing, if they knew what the consequences were?"

Stark nodded, then he asked, "What do *you* intend to do about the consequences?"

"Deal with them when we're back in port," Boxer answered.

Suddenly the phone rang.

Boxer was on his feet before Stark, and went to the phone.

The COMMO identified himself, and said, "Sir, we have picked up a message for us on an emergency frequency."

"Read it, but skip the intro."

"Aye, aye, sir... Request contact HQ immediately. Your situation is critical."

"Who signed it?"

"Admiral Hays, sir."

Boxer motioned to Stark to join him at the phone, and had the COMMO repeat the message.

Stark said, "I'd call him, if I were you... We're on our way back. They know where we are, and know that we're having some sort of problem with the drive system. They might know something about us that *we* don't know."

For several moments, Boxer considered Stark's last comment. "All right, radio HQ and patch me through to Admiral Hays. I'll be in my quarters."

"Aye, aye, sir," the COMMO responded.

Boxer replaced the phone, went back to the table, and finished the remainder of the coffee. "Come with me to my quarters," Boxer said. "I might need some quick advice."

Stark smiled. "I've never given you advice, and I don't intend to start now."

"What do you give me, then, when you *lecture* me?" Boxer asked as they left the wardroom."

"Suggestions... Food for thought."

"Is that what you've been giving me all these years?" Boxer asked, glancing sideways at Stark.

"I won't even dignify that question by attempting to answer it."

They were halfway to Boxer's cabin, when a sudden explosion threw both of them against the wall.

Instantly the klaxon began to scream.

Boxer pulled himself up, and as he started to reach down to Stark, another explosion dropped him to the floor.

"Get to the CR," Stark said. "I'll manage."

Boxer nodded, scrambled to his feet, and ran to the CR, where the SYS DISPLAY was filled with blinking red lights.

The WO switched on the 1MC. "Fire stations... Fire stations... All hands, fire stations..."

"I have the conn," Boxer said.

Borodine came running into the CR. "We have casualties," he said.

Boxer nodded and pointed to the Control Console. "Get damage reports."

Borodine immediately began contacting the boat's various operating divisional officers.

"Rupture in outer skin, section eighty-four," an officer of the watch reported.

Boxer watched the SYS DIS BD. Some of the red lights stopped blinking, and were replaced by green.

"Fire in reactor room," Borodine called out. "Fire fighters and DC control personnel are working on it."

The phone-to-boat's communications center rang.

A yeoman answered it, listened then said, "Admiral Boxer, it's the hookup with Admiral Hays."

"Put him on hold," Boxer answered. "No, tell him we have an emergency, and I will call him back."

"Aye, aye, sir," the man answered.

"Casualty report?" Boxer asked.

"One dead, three severely burned, five with broken bones of various kinds," Borodine reported.

"Could have been a lot worse," Boxer commented.

"Might still be," Borodine said.

Most of the red lights on the SYS DIS BD had turned green.

"Fire in the reactor room out," Borodine reported.

Boxer switched on the DAMAGE CONTROL ANALYSIS SYSTEM. System by system, the computer analyzed the electrical components, all valves, the flow of liquids and gasses through the various operating systems, and the surrounding air, for foreign gaseous components and extra high levels of oxygen, hydrogen, and carbon dioxide. The total analysis took five minutes, during which time Boxer checked the structural integrity of all of the boat's ribs and the inner skin, where the rupture had occurred.

"Structurally, we're okay," Boxer said.

"System check results coming up on monitor," Borodine told him.

The two of them watched the screen. System by system showed normal operation. Then suddenly, a flashing red warning circle came up on the color screen.

Excessive hydrogen in galley area, resulting from electrolysis of fresh water... Gas leaked into reactor area, and was ignited from an external source...

Boxer phoned the DCO, and told him what the DCAS revealed, then he said, "Shut down the galley, and tear it apart, until you find the source of the gas."

"Aye, aye, sir," the DCO answered.

"According to the duty roster, there were three men on duty in the reactor room at the time of the explosion," Borodine said, looking at another computer screen that displayed the watch.

Boxer switched on the 1MC, and ordered the men "to the CR on the double."

A moment later the phone rang. Borodine answered it, listened, and then said, "I will tell the Admiral."

"Tell me what?" Boxer questioned.

"One of the three men is dead, the other two are in critical condition," Borodine said.

Boxer pursed his lips, ran his hand over his jaw, and suddenly remembering that he'd left Stark sprawled out on the deck, he picked up the phone and called sick bay.

A corpsman answered.

"This is Admiral Boxer. I'd like to speak to the Comrade Doctor," he said.

"Sir, she's in surgery now," the man answered.

"Then, could you tell me Admiral Stark's condition?" Boxer asked.

"The Admiral is resting comfortably... He suffered a broken right arm."

"Thank you," Boxer said in a low voice, and put the phone down. "Stark suffered a broken right arm."

Borodine shook his head, but didn't say anything.

"I guess I better get back to Hays," Boxer said, and picked up the phone.

Within minutes Hays was on the line. "What kind of an emergency did you have?" he asked.

"A hydrogen explosion in the reactor area... One dead, three critical from third-degree burns, and an assortment of broken bones, including Stark's right arm."

"Everything under control now?" Hays asked.

"Yes, sir," Boxer answered.

"All right, now listen carefully... We know you're having drive shaft problems, and we know you're moving at a steady six knots, and that's the problem."

"I don't understand."

"You're creating a constant vibration frequency."

"Holy Christ!" Boxer exclaimed.

"We ran simulation tests," Hays said. "Your boat doesn't have the necessary equipment to run the same tests... We know you've got a readout recommending a speed of six knots."

Boxer turned to Borodine, "Reduce speed to three knots."

"I heard that," Hays said. "Vary your speed between three and nine knots... Don't run at any one speed for more than ten minutes. As soon as you clear the Davis Strait, we'll have a tug standing by to take you in tow."

"We'll operate under our own power, as long as we can," Boxer answered.

"All right, I don't want to have this discussion… It will be there if you need it."

"Send a frigate, too… Some of Fong Sh—"

"I know who you mean… You'll have your frigate," Hays said. Then, after a momentary pause, he said, "Good luck, Boxer."

"Thank you, sir," Boxer answered, and waited for Hays to click off, before he put the phone down. "This time, I'm damn glad I spoke to Hays," he said, looking at Borodine.

Borodine smiled. "I'm damn glad, too… We've had enough excitement around here for one day."

Boxer signaled the WO. "Take the conn," he said.

"Aye, aye, sir," the man answered.

"I'm going to visit the men in sick bay, then I'll be in my cabin," Boxer said.

"Yes, sir."

"I'll explain the speed changes," Borodine said.

"Thanks… You better get some rest, too."

"I will," Borodine answered.

Boxer nodded, left the captain's chair, and stretched. "Would you believe I ache all over?"

"Right now, I'd believe anything, even in miracles."

"Me, too… Especially now that we had one just happen, courtesy of Admiral Hays, the miracle man!"

"He'd love to hear you call him that," Borodine laughed.

"I bet!" Boxer answered, laughing, too…

CHAPTER 11

After a phone call from the coroner's office in Annapolis, telling him that the John Doe who had been burned alive three days before had been ID'd as Anthony Hale, a resident of Washington, Detective Green drove to meet with the coroner, in the hope that he might be able to come up with something that would help him identify the dead woman.

The coroner, Dr. John Shellby, was an avuncular man, who wore his glasses low on the bridge of his nose, and spoke with a distinct Southern drawl. Green judged that Shellby was about his age, give or take a year or two.

After the preliminary introductions, the two of them went down to the morgue, where Shellby opened up one of the refrigerator spaces, and pulled out a metal slab with a sheet-draped corpse on it, whose big right toe had a paper tag tied to it with "Anthony Hale" printed on it.

"You want to look?" Shellby said, his hand going to the top of the sheet.

Green shook his head. "No need to... Spoil what little breakfast I had, and ruin my appetite for lunch."

"If you're not used to it, it can do that to you," Shellby responded.

"How'd you make the ID so fast?"

"Luck." He smiled and pushed his glasses back a bit. "Luck... Know what the ancient Greeks and Romans called luck?"

"Fortuna... A lady, of course," Green answered, knowing that he'd surprise the Doctor. Then, with a wry smile, he added, "I've done some reading in my time."

Shellby nodded. "Lady Luck smiled on me, but not on Mr. Hale ... he carried one of his old army dog tags in his wallet. Though the heat had destroyed most of it, all but the last two digits of his serial number were intact. In a circle with a radius of a hundred miles, only three people had all of the other numbers in their army serial number. One was in Europe on a business trip, the second had died five years ago, and that left Mr. Hale. Then, from his dental work, we confirmed who he was."

Green nodded his head appreciatively.

"He's yours, if you want him... If we keep him here, he'll get the usual grand send-off to a pauper's grave."

"He'll enjoy the same if I take him."

"Any relatives?"

"None."

"You know that fire was so hot it melted all the glass in the car," Shellby said.

"I was hoping you might have found something."

"Nothing was left to find... By the way, did you get a make on the car?"

Green shook his head.

"Maybe you'd like to question the guy who spotted it?"

"I would."

"Good. You've just given me a legitimate reason for leaving this place," Shellby said, sliding Hale's body back into the refrigerator box and closing it. "A man should always have a legitimate reason for doing whatever he does. It follows the rule of cause and effect, and gives order to his life."

Green smiled.

"What was Hale into that got him incinerated?" Shellby asked, as they walked out to his car, a red Jeep 4X4.

"I don't really know... But my guess is that he was responsible for at least two murders: a woman, who jumped from his penthouse apartment, and a man, who was shot to death. These events occurred just hours after the two people were with Hale."

"You were hoping that I would have found something that connected him with one or both of the deaths?" Shellby asked, as he maneuvered out of the parking lot behind the city hospital, and into the flow of traffic.

"Yeah, that's what I was hoping," Green said.

Shellby reach over to the radio and switched it on. "I'm a longhair."

"It doesn't show, but so am I," Green answered.

The sound of a string quartet filled the jeep.

"Lunch after the meeting?" Shellby asked.

"That's fine with me."

For a few minutes neither one of them spoke, and giving himself up to the music, Green closed his eyes.

"You know the VIN was filed off the car's engine," Shellby said.

"I was sure it was," Green answered, still keeping his eyes closed.

"That was one hell of an expensive car to burn," Shellby commented.

Green opened his eyes. "I don't think the guys that Hale ran with have to worry much about money... I was up in his penthouse. He lived, very, very, very high on the hog."

"He may have lived that way, but he sure as hell didn't die that way, not that anyone does... But can you imagine what he must have experienced, when he found that he'd been locked in the car, before the flames got to him?"

"No, and to be frank, I wouldn't want to… I have enough to deal with my own reality, let alone attempting to imagine someone else's at a time like that."

Shellby turned on to the highway, and opened up to seventy. "We'll be there in about ten minutes," he said.

Green allowed himself to be caressed by the music, and before the piece was finished, Shellby had stopped the car in front of a small, neatly kept but weathered cottage.

"The man who lives here is something of recluse," Shellby explained, as he and Green walked toward the cottage. "Used to be a professor of English at the local junior college. Was on his way to being head of the department, from what I heard. Then, one day, for no apparent reason he resigned, left his wife of thirty-two years, and took off for about a year. When he came back, he moved into this place, and has been here ever since."

"What's he do for money?" Green asked.

"Raises herbs, and sells them to local restaurants. Does some crabbing for soft shells, and other odd jobs."

"Not much to keep going on, or for that matter, to even keep that battered old heap running," Green commented, as they reached the door.

Shellby leaned closer to Green. "Seems like —" The door suddenly opened, cutting him off.

The woman in the open doorway gave them a questioning look, frowned, and asked what they wanted.

"To see the man who lives here," Shellby said. "I believe his name is Branigan."

She nodded.

Green judged her to be about five-seven. She was somewhat big boned. Probably weighed about a hundred and thirty. But there wasn't any fat on her. Her body was about as well put together as it could have been. She had long, red hair, freckles on her face and neck, and lovely blue eyes. She wore a pair of faded but very clean jeans, and a white sweater that followed the curves of her breasts.

"I'd like to ask him some questions about the men he saw a few days ago," Green said, showing her his gold shield.

Her eyes met his.

"Ian is in town," she said. "Maybe I can help you. I was with him the day he saw the men."

Green glanced at Shellby, and said, "You never said anything about another person —"

"He said that he was the only one," Shellby answered.

Green looked back at the woman, nodded, and said, "I'd appreciate it if you'd tell us exactly what you saw."

She stepped back from the open doorway, and said, "You might as well come in."

The two men followed her in. She lead them to a small living room, furnished with a couch, two club chairs, a TV, an elaborate sound system, and floor-to-ceiling shelves crammed with books.

Green and Shellby settled on the couch, while she sat down on the edge of one of the easy chairs. Clasping her hands together in her lap, she kept herself rigid.

"I appreciate this," Green said, hoping to make the woman feel less uncomfortable.

"Ian and I were out for a walk… We'd just come around the bend in the road just before the house, when we saw this car, with its hood up, and a man looking at the engine. We stopped. Ian doesn't ordinarily become involved with strangers, but this time, he said that maybe we should offer to help. I agreed. But at that moment a black Olds—"

"Are you sure of the make and color of the car?" Green asked.

"Yes... It pulled up some distance behind the white Mercedes — that was the car whose hood was open — and the next moment, the man who was looking under the hood, took several steps backward and ran to the other car. There were three men in the car, the driver, the man alongside of him, and a man in the back.

"The car started up, and by the time it made a U-turn, the man who was running toward it, reached it. The rear, right door was opened, and he jumped in.

"We were so surprised, we stopped. Then suddenly, Ian pulled me down to the ground, and the car blew up... We didn't realize there was anyone in it, until some other detectives came around and told us." She ended by saying, "That's all I have to tell." Then she uttered a loud sigh of relief.

"You couldn't see into the Mercedes, because the hood was up?" Green said, purposely phrasing his question as a statement, to make it easier for her to answer it.

She nodded, then said, "The black car was already moving when the man jumped into it."

"Did you get a good look at any of them?"

"No."

"Your husband —" Green began.

"Ian and I live together," she said, looking straight at him.

"Mr. Branigan seemed to know that there was going to be an explosion," Green said.

"Yes... He said later that the man would not have run away, if something terrible wasn't going to happen... And at the moment, the only thing he could guess was going to happen, was that there would be an explosion."

"It was a good guess," Shellby said, breaking a long silence.

"I can't tell you anything else, and I don't think Ian could either," she said.

"Thank you, Miss —"

"Miss Field," she responded, as she got to her feet.

Green nodded to Shellby, and the two of them followed her to the door.

She opened the door, and stepped back to let them pass.

"Again, thank you," Green said, taking hold of her hand, and shaking it.

Moments later, Green and Shellby were out of the house, and on their way to the car. Before they reached it, they heard the door close.

"You think that bit about the make and the color of the car will help?" Shellby asked, as he slid behind the wheel of his 4X4.

"Every little bit helps," Green answered, then he commented, "Miss Fields is a very attractive woman."

"She certainly is," Shellby said, turning on the radio, after he'd made a U-turn.

"What did you start to tell me about Ian?" Green asked.

"I can't remember."

"I'd commented that he didn't seem to earn enough…"

"Yes, yes… I remember now… Well, this is really the strange part… There are rumors that he's written several books, and is well known in New York publishing circles. He has a mail box in the local post office under the name of Charles Koral."

Green smiled.

"What's funny?"

"Not funny — strange," Green answered. Anticipating the doctor's next question, he said, "We're strange… People are strange…"

"I may be strange, but I am also hungry," Shellby said.

"So am I… Have you any place in mind where we could go to eat? A place that wouldn't mind if we dawdled over lunch, and where the food is not just good, but *very* good?"

"I sure do, and we'll have a beautiful waterside view, too," Shellby answered.

"Good," Green answered. "Very good." Then he said, "I guess if people weren't strange, we'd be out of business… Lots of us would be out of business, including the Charles Korals of the world… But I'd have to say that finding that woman there was certainly strange, wouldn't you say?"

"Yes, I would," Shellby answered.

"I wonder what she sees in him?"

"Probably his strangeness," Shellby answered, smiling wryly.

Green glanced at him and guffawed. "You certainly have an analytical mind," he said. "A strange one at that."

CHAPTER 12

The weather began to moderate as the SSN-S1 sailed slowly south along the west coast of Greenland, though by comparison to the weather further south, it still would be considered extremely harsh.

Boxer, when he wasn't with Borodine, spent most of his time resting, reading, and writing a report to William Smith, the Secretary of the Navy, and to Admiral Hays, about the "hot zone" in the North Pacific, and its impact on the ecology of the various oceans of the world.

Borodine was preparing a similar report to his superiors in Moscow, and they frequently discussed the situation to pool their extensive knowledge of the oceans.

On a particularly clear night, the aurora borealis shimmered across the sky, and Boxer, who had heard the men speak about it, invited Ilia up to the bridge to see it.

Shades of green, pink, and lavender moved curtainlike across the sky, giving it an even more magical appearance than it had with the diamond-point glistening of the stars.

Ilia whispered, "It's too beautiful to describe... It's like listening to Mozart's music."

Boxer smiled and nodded.

She looked up at him, and said, "This is the first time I've been outside since we left Norfolk, and it feels wonderful to be able to breathe real air, not rescrubbed air... You know there *is* a difference."

He said, "If there is, I wouldn't know it. But maybe, up *here* there is a difference." And he gently tapped the side of her head with his gloved hand.

"You're too used to the other kind to recognize it," she said.

"Probably," Boxer answered.

"It's almost impossible to believe that there is so much beauty in such a harsh environment, and after —" She paused. "I'm not sure *danger* is the right word, but I can't think of any other... After the danger we've been through, so many times, I was afraid that — well, you, too, were probably afraid that we wouldn't make it home."

Boxer laughed. "I was too worried to be afraid."

"That's just a dodge... Another way of saying that you were just as afraid as the rest of us."

"More," Boxer said, his tone turning serious. "I have all of you to be afraid for."

"I know... You and Comrade Admiral Borodine are like mother hens."

"Mother hens!" Boxer exclaimed. "Mother hens! Wait until I tell your Comrade Admiral what you really think of him."

"If the two of you weren't like that, neither of you would be the man you are."

"That's an odd way of putting it," Boxer said.

"Odd or not, it is the way it is," Ilia replied.

The aurora dimmed, and Boxer suggested they go down to the wardroom for a cup of hot coffee.

"I'd like that, but I'll only have a cup of hot chocolate."

Boxer helped her down through the hatch. At the bottom of the ladder, they were suddenly face to face and together. He had his arms around her.

She did not move.

He wanted to press her to him, and put his lips against hers. Suddenly, she said, "I really would like that hot chocolate."

He stepped away from her. "Yes, certainly."

A few minutes later, they sat across from each other at a small table. Ilia had her mug of hot chocolate, and Boxer his mug of steaming, black coffee.

"Comrade Admiral Borodine has told me that the two of you are going to recommend that destruction of the hot zone, and the criminal prosecution of those responsible for creating it," she said.

Boxer nodded. "With everyone so concerned about the environment, I don't think we'll have too much difficulty convincing our respective governments to do something about it."

"And what do *you* think should be done?"

"Seal it," Boxer said. "Just dump a few million tons of rock over it, so that it can't escape into the ocean."

"And you and the Comrade Admiral will do it?" she questioned, as she held her mug of hot chocolate in front of her.

Boxer shook his head. "No, we'll leave that to other people. Igor wants to spend time with his family, and now that he is a multimillionaire, I think that he wants to enjoy the good life, whatever that means."

She laughed. "In America it means having everything you want. Living the way people do on TV."

"And in your country?"

She shrugged. "Not like in America, but very, very well, indeed," she said. Then she asked, "What will you do?"

"Rest. I have a great deal of thinking to do," Boxer said. "I have the feeling that I have a lot of catching up, and please don't ask me what I mean by that, because I will tell you I don't really know."

Ilia laughed. "You're in a universal club with a membership of most of the people who are living, and probably those who have lived, and those who are yet to be born."

"Too heavy for my poor brain to deal with now," Boxer said. "Much too heavy."

"Well, I have some patients to take care of," Ilia said.

"And I have to make some checks in the CR," Boxer responded.

They stood up simultaneously.

"Thanks again for inviting me up to the bridge."

"The pleasure was mine."

"And mine, too," she answered.

For a moment, neither of them moved.

"I will never forget it," Ilia whispered.

"Nor will I," Boxer answered, engaging her eyes with his.

"I better go," she said in a low, throaty voice.

Boxer nodded…

Green was at his desk riffling through papers. He hated doing any kind of paperwork, and either postponed it as long as possible, or found some excuse not to do it at all. It didn't matter whether it was writing checks for his monthly bills, or writing a report. He hated them with an equal passion. He was just about to start writing his report on the Hale case. The death of the Jane Doe and the murder of Commander Negron — though tied to each other — still didn't give him either Negron's hit man or why the woman went out of the window, or who torched Hale. Then his phone rang.

"Detective Captain Green here," he said, glad to be distracted from what he was about to do.

"Cap'n there's a woman out here, Kate Brennan, a writer."

"Maybe she wants to write my reports," Green said, looking at a roach that just climbed up onto the top of the desk, and was waving its antennae around to get a fix on something.

The man on the other end was used to Green's comments, and ignoring him, he continued. "Says she's lookin' for her friend... Says that when she went to where her friend lives, the security man said her friend never lived there."

"Turn her — what's her name?"

"Miss Kate Brennan."

"Whatever... Turn her over to — Who was her friend?" Green asked, suddenly leaning forward and planting his elbows on the desk.

"A woman... That's why I thought you'd be interested. That Jane Doe —"

"Yeah, yeah... If we get a make, I'll buy you a beer, Charley... Send her in." Green dropped the phone down into its hold, gathered the papers on his desk together and worked them between his hands until they were even, and after he brushed the roach off, he placed them on the side of the desk, where the roach had been. Then he leaned against the back of his swivel chair, and waited for Miss Kate Brennan... Maybe, Fortuna would be on his side of the game today...

He stood up the moment she appeared in the doorway. She was a knockout, complete with black leather miniskirt, a tight-fitting blue sweater that matched her blue eyes, and long, red hair that cascaded off her shoulders. He introduced himself.

"Kate Brennan," she said, offering her hand.

Green shook it, gestured to the chair alongside the desk, and as both of them sat down, he asked, "What can I do for you?"

"Find my girlfriend," she said, her blue eyes boring into him.

"What's your girlfriend's name?" Green asked, now very much aware of the lilac scent of her perfume, and the upper reaches of her very sheer, black pantyhose-covered thighs.

"Lill — Lillian Forbes. At least, that's the name she uses."

"The name she uses?"

"For business purposes."

"And what is her business?" Green asked.

"She runs an escort service."

He raised his eyebrows questioningly.

"All right, she's a call girl," Kate said. "But she was —"

"Do you know if she knew a man named Anthony Hale?"

Now she raised *her* eyebrows. "How did you know that?"

Green took a deep breath and slowly exhaled, then he said, "Your girl friend — Lillian Forbes — jumped out of Hale's apartment a few nights ago."

"Oh my God!" she exclaimed, putting her hand to her mouth. The redhead squinched her eyes shut to fight back the tears.

"Would you like some water?" Green asked.

Kate nodded and managed a thank you.

Green left the room, went over to another detective in the squad room, and said, "We got an ID on the woman who went out of Hale's window. Name is Lillian Forbes. Same woman that Negron went to see before he got himself blown away."

"All we have are stiffs... Now what?" the detective asked.

"Now, I get a cup of water for that beautiful woman in my office," Green said, and headed straight for the water cooler.

By the time he returned with the cup of water, Kate had regained her composure. But she took the water, drank some of it, and said, "The security people where she lived told me she never lived there."

"Are you sure it wasn't a phony address?" Green asked.

"I was in her apartment," Kate answered.

"I'll check it out... Now, tell me, Ms. Brennan, did Lillian ever tell you anything about Hale?"

She thought for a moment. "Nothing —"

"What?"

"Well, he got her clients."

"He was her pimp?"

"They were business associates of his."

"And you wouldn't happen to know what business he was in?"

"Something to do with waste disposal... Lillian was never too clear about it."

"Hale is dead, too... Burned alive in a locked car."

Again Kate gasped. But this time there weren't any tears. This time she asked if Green had any idea why Lillian had leaped out of the window.

Shaking his head, Green said, "Not yet... Her body was pretty well smashed up when it struck the ground. The coroner is still working on it."

"Lillian wasn't the suicidal type... Are you sure she jumped, and wasn't pushed?"

Green shrugged. "The experts say that her trajectory indicates that she leaped."

"Something must have been more frightening to her than death," Kate said.

Green agreed.

"I guess each of us came out of this meeting with something," Kate said. "You were able to identify a Jane Doe, and I found out that the Jane Doe was my girlfriend." She stood up.

"Are you going to claim the body?"

"Yes... I'll have it cremated."

"Doesn't she have any relatives?"

"She was an only child, and her mother is dead, and she had no idea where her father was."

"I'll have the body released to you, as soon as the coroner is finished with it."

"Thank you," Kate said, extending her hand across the desk. Green shook it.

She let go of his hand. "I want you to get the people responsible for Lillian's death."

"I'll certainly try."

"Not good enough, Captain... Get them," Kate said, her voice suddenly going hard. "Get them... I'm going to write about Lillian and Hale..."

"I hope you're not threatening me, Ms. Brennan?" Green said.

"No... I am just telling you that I'm not going to get off your case, until you arrest the person or persons responsible for Lillian's death."

"That *is* a threat!"

"No, it is a statement of fact, Captain. A statement of fact," Kate said. Then she smiled and turned.

CHAPTER 13

"Link up at fourteen hundred," Commander Sarkis said, as he scanned the NAVSYS display, where three ships — two frigates and one oceangoing tug — were on station at 60 north lat., 50 west long.

Boxer nodded. He'd been in radio contact with the skipper, Commander Alberto Maggellen, aboard the frigate, *W. W. Johnson*, for the last forty-eight hours. The three ships had arrived in the vicinity twenty hours before, when the weather had been fairly good. But now the barometer was beginning to drop, and where those ships were, at the Atlantic end of the strait, a Force 5 gale was already blowing.

"I'd like to tell them to move south out of the storm, but we might need them," Boxer said, more to himself than to anyone in the CR.

"Maybe we could send the frigates south," Borodine suggested.

Boxer turned. "I didn't even know you were here," he said. Then he added, "You heard me?"

"Yes."

"What do you think?"

"We might need all the help we can get," Borodine said. "If that gale is blowing when we link up with them — well, we might need them."

Boxer agreed. "But the men aboard those ships must be as unhappy as hell."

"Wouldn't you be, if you were in their place?"

"I'd curse everyone and everything that put me where I was," Boxer answered with a grin.

"So would I," Borodine said.

"Well, it looks as if everything is under control here, so I'll leave and visit Stark. He doesn't like being in sick bay, but Ilia — I mean Comrade Dr. Ioff wants him there until we reach port."

Borodine suggested that he, too, visit Stark.

"I'm sure he'll be glad to see you," Boxer answered, as they left the CR.

Just before they reached sick bay, Borodine said, "Jack, I'd like to have a few words with you in private."

"My cabin?" Boxer offered.

"Mine is closer," Borodine said.

"Yours," Boxer responded.

Borodine lead the way, opened the door to his cabin, and gestured Boxer in.

The cabin was identical to his. Same high-tech equipment, same bunk, same desk and chair. The only difference was that Borodine had pictures of his wife and child on the desk and on the walls. And he also had a compact disc player, a small collection of discs, and a dozen books on a shelf, including the complete works of Shakespeare and the King James version of the Bible.

Boxer dropped onto one of the chairs.

Borodine took the other, and said, "To begin with, let me say that I know this is none of my business."

"*But*," Boxer commented.

"*But* you are my closest friend, even though we might disagree on some things, we usually are — how do you put it?"

"See eye to eye."

"Yes, we see eye to eye on most things," Borodine said. "Most of the time, where we didn't see eye to eye, a woman was involved, and, now, a woman is involved again. Ilia —"

"You're right, it's none of your business," Boxer said. "But now that you brought the subject up, let me tell you that we are good friends."

"Just good friends?"

Boxer pressed his hands together.

"Jack, she's also my adopted sister," Borodine said. "I know you well enough to know that you will not be content to be just good friends."

"Has it ever occurred to you, that Ilia might want a much more meaningful relationship than just being good friends?" Boxer asked.

"I'm sure she does. I'm sure she's ready to fall in love again, marry, and — But that's not the kind of meaningful relationship you're talking about, is it?"

Boxer was silent.

"I didn't think it was," Borodine commented.

Boxer was about to admit that he *had* been thinking about marriage again, but the scream of the klaxon cut him off. Then Sarkis came on the 1MC. "Battle stations... All hands, battle stations... Now hear this, all hands, battle stations."

"What the hell!" Boxer exclaimed, getting to his feet.

Borodine was already up and at the door.

The two of them left the cabin at a run, heading for the CR.

"Target, zero eight five... Range, twelve miles... Speed, zero six knots... Depth, ninety feet... Course, zero ten," Sarkis reported.

"I have the conn," Boxer said... The target was coming up on their starb'd bow.

"Aye, aye, sir," Sarkis answered.

"Have communications check with Commander Maggellen whether or not they had any sonar contacts," Boxer said.

"Aye, aye, sir," Sarkis answered.

"Borodine, arm and prepare to launch the submersible," Boxer said, turning on the UWIS.

Borodine switched on the 1MC, and said, "Arm and prepare to launch submersible two... Arm and prepare to launch submersible two."

The communications phone rang. Sarkis picked it up, then said, "Commander Maggellen reports negative."

"Roger that," Boxer said.

"Do we have an ID on the target?" Borodine asked.

"Getting it now," Sarkis answered.

"Why didn't it come up when contact was first made?"

"It was not in the primary database," Sarkis answered. "We had to record the sound, transmit via the polar satellite to our HQ database... We're lucky that the satellite was still in position for us to transmit and receive. Another two minutes and it would have been out of range."

Borodine looked at the display monitor:

Sea Wolf type submarine Nuclear powered... Maximum speed of surface 20 knots... Maximum speed submerged... 35 knots Armed with six standard type torpedoes... Cruising range, 400,000 miles before refueling... Sold to developing countries.

"Some of Fong Shun Un's friends," Borodine commented.

Boxer looked at the screen. "I never did think it was a good idea to sell our old weapons, or some of our new ones, for that matter, to developing countries."

"Especially when you have to face them," Borodine said.

Another phone rang, and a yeoman answered it.

"Submersible armed and ready to launch," the man reported.

"We'll start feeding it data from here until it's in shooting range, then it will rely on its own navigational and fire control systems," Boxer said.

Sarkis relayed the information to the submersible's skipper, Lieutenant Christopher Dee, while Borodine made the necessary adjustments of the NAVSYS and FC switch settings.

"My guess is that her electronics have been considerably upgraded, and are probably equal to ours... She might even have a UWIS aboard," Boxer said.

Borodine nodded. "A possibility. But not one that I would want to think about."

"They can outrun us, except when they set up for a shoot; then they must cut their speed to six knots."

"And they're not counting on having to deal with the submersible," Borodine said.

"We'll bring the submersible in close... I want their sonar to pick it up, and if they *do* have some form of UWIS, to see it. It will throw them off, and maybe the UWIS will be able to launch a killing salvo."

"We'll head the submersible straight in?"

"Straight in at flank speed," Boxer said.

Borodine relayed the instructions to Dee. Then, switching on the 1MC, he said, "All hands, now hear this... All hands, now hear this... Stand by to launch submersible..."

"Launch bay flooding," Sarkis reported, viewing the launch bay on a TV monitor.

"Turn on power," Borodine told Dee.

"Launch bay flooded," Sarkis said.

"Opening launch bay doors," Borodine said, pressing a red control button.

"Doors fully open," Sarkis reported, after ten seconds.

"Full power," Borodine ordered.

"Submersible launched."

"Closing launch bay doors," Borodine said, pressing a black control button.

"Launch bay doors closed and sealed," Sarkis said.

Boxer reached over to the audio control panel on the MCC, and reset a switch that put voice communication between the submersible and the SSN-S1 over the PA system.

"All systems green," Dee reported. "Flank speed... Target dead ahead."

"That's going to give them something to think about," Boxer said.

"Maybe make them give some serious thought to turning around, and getting the hell out of there," Borodine said with an impish smile.

"Target turning," the SO reported.

"They've made contact with you, Dee... Stay with them," Boxer said, watching the three-dimensional shapes move on the TDS.

"Wilco," Dee responded.

"They're diving!" Borodine exclaimed.

"Coming into switch-over range," Dee reported.

"Switch over now," Borodine said.

"NAV and FC systems green," Dee reported. "Depth, six hundred."

"They have a thousand-foot floor," Boxer said.

"Preparing to fire," Dee said. A moment passed, then he said, "Two darts away!"

Boxer watched the darts streak down toward their target.

"Got 'em!" Dee exclaimed.

On the screen the target fell apart, and the next instant the muffled boom of the explosion rolled over the SSN-S1.

"They never had a chance," Dee said.

"Return to base," Boxer ordered. Turning to Sarkis, he said, "Secure from General Quarters."

"Aye, aye, sir," Sarkis answered, adding, "Nothing like a little action to make things interesting."

"I could have done without it," Boxer answered. Leaving the captain's chair, he said to Borodine, "This time we're closer to my cabin."

"Do you want to pick up the conversation?"

"Yes," Boxer said, and, after returning the conn to Sarkis, he led the way out of the CR.

When they reached the cabin, Borodine sat on the extra chair, and Boxer took the one at the desk.

"You're my friend, my best friend," Borodine began. "But I feel a certain responsibility toward Ilia... Do you understand that?"

"Certainly," Boxer answered.

"She is a —"

"A beautiful, clever woman... What if I told you, I might consider being serious."

"Serious?"

"Marriage," Boxer said.

Borodine gave him a questioning look.

"I'm even thinking about resigning," Boxer said, getting up and perching on the edge of the gray metal desk. "I'm at sixes and sevens about practically everything. I'm no longer satisfied with what I do, or for that matter, with what I *have* done."

"I, too, sometimes feel that way," Borodine admitted. "But I have my family, and I have been given various other assignments."

"Including a prison stay," Boxer said.

"A slight detour," Borodine answered with a wry smile.

"I want to lead a more normal life... Well, maybe not normal as most people define it, but I want to do some of the things I've always wanted to do."

"Most men would gladly trade places with either of us," Borodine said.

Boxer nodded. "I know that, and I probably would go off my rocker if I had to live the way other men do... But I'm not really asking for their lifestyle... I'm asking for one of my own that is not connected to the Company, or the Navy. I have all the money — more money than I'll ever be able to use in one lifetime. But I would like to enjoy it, while I'm in this life."

Borodine nodded. "I can understand that, too... Now that I have money, too, I have been thinking along similar lines."

"And as far as my relationship with Ilia goes — well, it really hasn't gone anywhere, yet... We're good friends."

"Somewhat more than just good friends, Jack. I can see it in her eyes, when she looks at you."

Boxer laughed. "She does have beautiful eyes."

"And I can hear it in your voice, when you say her name."

Boxer waved his friend's comments aside.

"Just think before you do anything that might hurt her," Borodine said. "She's a good person, Jack."

"I know she is."

Borodine stood up. "All this talking has made me thirsty. How about joining me for coffee?"

"Good idea!" Boxer said, launching himself off the edge of the desk. "You know, maybe the two of us could go into some kind of business together... What do you think about that possibility?" he asked, as they left his cabin.

Borodine laughed. "We're not businessmen... We're admirals. We'd have to find something that a pair of admirals could do, when they no longer want to be admirals."

Boxer put his arm around his friend's shoulders. "You have a way of putting things, Igor, that's totally unique."

"Being unique can hardly be called a business, especially since only one of us is, and there are two of us."

They looked at each other and guffawed...

CHAPTER 14

The SSN-S1 rendezvoused with its escort force, and continued its slow progress south. The weather moderated, and by the time they'd reached 50 north latitude, Boxer, Borodine, Ioff, and any of the men who had been injured, were airlifted by choppers to Gander, Newfoundland, and flown by navy transports to Washington.

A limo was waiting at the airport for Boxer and Borodine, and they were driven to Langley, where Olsen, Smith, and Hays were waiting for them.

After the customary greetings, and as soon as everyone was comfortably seated around the coffee table, Olsen didn't waste any time. "Aside from the success of your salvage operation, Admirals, you deliberately disobeyed an order," he said.

Boxer looked at Borodine, nodded, and said, as he and Borodine stood up, "Excuse us, gentlemen... Neither of us have any intention of listening to Mr. Olsen's criticism of our behavior. We followed the rules that any mariner would in a similar situation. Mr. Olsen, your order was superseded by the more humane, and much older, law of the sea." He and Borodine started to walk toward the door.

"You can't just walk out!" Olsen shouted.

"I did it before... Remember? And I am doing it again," Boxer answered, without turning. "This time —"

"Jack, be reasonable," Hays said. "Olsen doesn't understand why you did —"

Boxer stopped, turned, and looked at the men. Hays and Olsen were on their feet, and Smith, the Secretary of the Navy, had remained seated. "All right, we'll come back, and tell you what we found."

It took a few moments for them to regain their former seats. Then Boxer said, "By the time we reached the downed boat, her entire crew was dead. They all died from massive doses of radiation... Radiation that came from an external source... The boat had explored a hot zone in the North Pacific, a place where nuclear waste is being dumped, a place that will, if given enough time, succeed in poisoning the oceans of the world."

"Come, come, Admiral, aren't you exaggerating the situation?" Smith said.

"We have the boat's log," Borodine said.

"Still, you yourself haven't examined the so-called hot zone," Smith said, and Olsen agreed with him.

Then Smith said, "I trust you have made all of this information available in a report?"

"I have, and so has Comrade Admiral Borodine," Boxer said.

"Is it possible that the boat's skipper was covering up —"

"The boat's reactor system was totally operational," Borodine said.

"We have it on very good authority that your government had the boat destroyed," Smith said. "Why would they do that?"

Borodine shrugged. "I can not answer that," he responded. Then he added, "But I will certainly try to find out."

"If and when you do, I hope you will tell us, that is, of course, as long as your telling us does not violate your government's security regulations."

"Suppose this hot zone exists, what would you do about it?" Olsen asked.

"First, let's get something straight here, before we go any further. The hot zone does exist. Second, I am going to try to have this government form a coalition of nations to destroy it, and make sure that the illegal dumping of nuclear, and/or chemical waste is banned, and that some sort of international control is set up to prevent it."

Even Borodine was surprised by Boxer's response.

"Admiral Borodine, do you share Admiral Boxer's views?" Olsen asked.

"Yes," he answered.

"Am I to understand that you've included these recommendations in your report?" Hays asked.

"Yes, sir. I have spelled out those recommendations in detail."

"And you have done the same, Comrade Admiral Borodine?" Hays asked.

"Yes, to my surprise, this is an aspect of the report that we did not discuss," Borodine answered, smiling at Boxer. "We have very similar ideas about this matter."

"Interesting," Olsen commented.

"Then I will expect your report —" Smith began.

"Admiral Hays will have my report by the middle of next week," Boxer said. "He will send it up through channels."

"Aside from the difficulties you encountered, is there anything else you want to report?" Olsen asked.

Boxer told them about the structural damage, the cause of the fire, and that the drive shaft was defective.

"As soon as the boat comes in, she will undergo exhaustive repairs," Smith said.

Hays added, "She will even be fitted with a weapon system that will give her the same firepower as an attack submarine... Really more, with the two submersibles and the added gunship on her afterdeck, which will be able to be launched from periscope depth."

Boxer nodded his head approvingly.

"Well, gentlemen, just how much did each of you earn on this salvage expedition?"

"Twenty million," Boxer answered.

"That isn't bad for a few weeks of work," Smith said.

"Every cent of it was earned," Borodine responded. "You seem to have forgotten that we took casualties, Mr. Secretary."

"I didn't mean to underestimate —"

"Leave it alone," Boxer snapped. "Our share is our share, whether we came by it with ease, or with difficulty... And now, if you gentlemen don't have any other questions, or complaints—" For several moments, he looked squarely at Olsen. "None. Good. We will go, then."

"How much is Boxer really worth?" Olsen asked, after Boxer and Borodine had left.

"He's a very, very wealthy man," Hays answered.

"And where did all of the money come from?" Olsen questioned.

"He was left money, Admiral Stark has willed him other monies, and his investments keep earning more."

Olsen made a humming sound, but didn't say anything.

"Do you think that the two of them are serious about urging the government to take action against this hot zone, as they call it?" Smith asked.

"I can only tell you that I've never known Boxer to say that he was going to do something, then fail to do it," Hays answered. "He's one man — no, I'll rephrase that — he and Borodine are two men whose word you can absolutely depend on."

"I imagine that's why they're such good officers," Smith said.

"That's why they do the kind of work they do," Olsen added. "I don't care for either of them, but they get the job done."

"And they do it under circumstances that would cower the most audacious officers we have," Hays replied.

"What makes it possible for them to accomplish the seemingly impossible?"

Hays smiled, shrugged his shoulders, and said, "If I knew what it was, I'd try to have it manufactured, so that I could give it to every man in the Navy."

"And every man in the Company," Olsen said. "I might even take it myself."

Hays shook his head. "On some men," he laughed, "it probably just wouldn't work."

Boxer went directly to his hotel after he left Borodine at the Russian Embassy, and phoned Ilia at her apartment. The phone rang twice before she picked it up.

"Boxer, here," he said, before she had a chance to speak.

"You promised me that you would rest," she said.

"News travels fast, especially when you have Igor to deliver it," Boxer said, walking the length of the bedroom with the cordless phone in his hand.

"Jack, you don't even know who will be battling," she said.

He laughed. "That's what makes this so interesting... But I didn't call you to discuss my future. I called to invite you out for dinner, a real dinner, in a real restaurant."

"I'm sorry, Jack, but I must attend an official function at the Embassy," she said. "There isn't any way I can get out of it."

"Tomorrow night, then?"

"Yes."

"Any particular restaurant that you'd like to go to?"

She was silent for a moment.

"Go ahead, tell me," he urged.

"There's a North Mongolian restaurant in Fairfax —"

He laughed, "North Mongolian?"

"You choose then," she said.

"No, no. If that's where you want to go, that's where we'll go. I'll pick you up about seven."

"Seven," she answered.

"See you," Boxer said, and returned the phone to its place. Then he went into the bathroom to shave and shower. But when he looked at himself in the mirror, he suddenly decided that he was tired of shaving, and just showered. The hot water pouring over him felt very good; and after toweling himself dry, he returned to the bedroom, and put on clean skivvies. Feeling tired, he pulled back the bedspread and stretched out on the bed for a nap. Later, he intended to visit Stark, who was being held overnight for observation at the Bethesda Naval Hospital, to make sure that the bones in his arm were healing properly. But now he suddenly felt drained of energy.

He fell asleep wondering about how it would feel to hang glide, to feel every change in the air currents, to hear only the wind, and the sound made by the flow of his own blood...

The ringing of the phone destroyed the sleep he'd entered. He picked up the phone, and before he could speak, the woman on the other end said, "Kate Brennan here!"

"You have a knack for calling me when I'm in bed," he said, pushing himself up and leaning against the headboard.

"I have other knacks, too," she said seductively.

"That you do... That you do."

"Aren't you going to ask me how I knew you were back?" she questioned.

"You're not going to believe this, but I don't really give a damn," Boxer answered.

"What are those lines — 'Home is the sailor, home from the sea' — I thought of them when I found out you were back, they in turn brought to mind another line, not verbatim, mind you, but the general idea is that there's something a sailor can only get in port." She laughed, then asked, "I'm sure we both have a good idea of what that is... I'll make you an offer you can't refuse: I'll take you to dinner, then after dinner, I'll take you to bed. How's that for erring on the side of being a generous, good-hearted woman?"

"If it were any other woman, I'd have to admit it way beyond being a generous, good-hearted woman. But since the offer came from you, there's got to be more than either an appetite for food or sex, each of which you must have satisfied while I was away."

"Jack, how could you say that about me?" she said, altering the tone of her voice to echo her bruised feelings. "I pined for you, for your embrace!" She couldn't continue, and burst into laughter.

Boxer laughed, too. Then he said, "Certainly, I'll go. I couldn't refuse such a generous offer of sex and food."

"The food comes first."

"Absolutely."

"But there *is* something I want to talk to you about, Jack."

"Not the book, not my biography," Boxer said.

"No... A friend of mine — you met her once, a beautiful blonde —"

"She was with that flashy-looking guy, wasn't she?"

"Yes, that was her."

"*Was* her?"

"Lillian is dead, and so is that guy, Anthony — Tony — Hale."

Boxer gave a long, low whistle. "A double suicide?" he questioned. That was the first thing that came to his mind.

"No. She jumped, or was pushed out of his penthouse window, and he was burned to death in a car."

"Well, at least we'll have an interesting conversation, even if the food and sex is bad," Boxer said, trying to inject a bit of humor into the situation.

She was quick on the uptake. "The food may be bad, but with me in bed with you, how can the sex be bad?"

"My mistake. I humbly apologize."

"Apology accepted... Do you want to drive, or shall I?"

"Where are we going?"

"Don't be too nosey."

"All right, rather than have you give me directions, you drive," Boxer said.

"Good. I'll be by about eight," she said.

"I'll be downstairs," he told her.

"I'm glad you're back," she said. "I missed you."

"I'm glad I'm back, too," he answered, then he added, "I missed you, too, Kate."

"That's good to hear, Jack. See you," she said, and clicked off.

Boxer put the phone down, and said aloud, "The strange thing is, that I did miss you, Kate." He hadn't realized how much he had missed her, until he heard her voice...

Smith left the meeting, and drove from the Company Headquarters in Langley to the Washington International Airport, where he purchased a round-trip ticket for the shuttle flight to New York. Then he made a quick call to New York, depositing the required amount in the coin box instead of using his credit card.

Immediately after the first ring, a woman answered. "World Wide Shipping, may I help you?"

"Mr. Arkady Tosenko, please."

"Who shall I say is calling?"

"Bly, Captain Bly," Smith said, using his code name.

Moments later a man said, "I didn't expect to hear from you so quickly."

"I'm on my way up... We have a major problem... Have someone meet me at LaGuardia in an hour and a half... I don't want to wait... I must be back in Washington early this evening for a reception at the Russian Embassy."

"Everything will be taken care of," Tosenko answered.

Smith waited until he heard the click at the other end before he put the phone down, and headed for the bar. He still had a half hour before boarding, and he needed a drink...

Boxer tried, but couldn't get back to sleep, or even back to that relaxed state he had been in before Kate had called. He got out of the bed, slipped into a pair of slacks, put on a checkered flannel shirt, and tossing a light denim jacket across his shoulders, he left his suite and headed for the elevator... It was always difficult to make the change from living on the edge to a daily rhythm that was something near normal.

Before the elevator came, he was joined by an elderly couple, who lived in a suite down the hall. He nodded to them, and they returned the courtesy. And then a woman, whom he had never seen before, joined them. He judged her to be in her late thirties. He nodded and smiled at her.

She ignored him.

The elevator came, and stepping aside, he said, "After you."

The elderly couple moved into the elevator car, the woman followed, and as Boxer started into the car, she said, "I think you had better use the service elevator." Then she pressed the door control button.

Boxer stopped the doors from closing, entered the elevator, and said, "I suggest you go to Bloomingdale's and buy a new set of manners."

The elderly couple laughed, and said, "Admiral, it's good to have you back."

"Admiral!" the woman exclaimed.

"Admiral Jack Boxer," the elderly gentlemen said. "He lives here."

Boxer grinned at the woman.

"But he's dressed —"

"As the old expression goes, never judge a book by its cover, and, if I might add, a person by what he or she wears," Boxer said.

"I'm terribly sorry," the woman said, as the car reached the lobby, and its doors opened.

Boxer nodded, and let the couple and the woman precede him into the lobby.

"Please, I really would like to apologize," the woman said, as he came out of the car.

"You already have... But you could tell me your name."

"Mrs. Constance Wright."

"Well, Mrs. Wright, I'm glad to meet you," he said, shaking her hand.

"Are you going out like that?"

"Like what?"

"With just that light jacket... It's only forty outside."

"Mrs. Wright, where I've just come from, forty degrees would be a heatwave," Boxer said with a laugh. "Now, if you'll excuse me..."

"Won't you even let me buy you a drink?" she asked, looking straight at him.

"Another time," he said, aware of the eye contact between them. "Right now, it's important that I get out and walk."

"That's exactly what I was going to do. I just got bored with staying indoors, and decided the best tonic for that condition is a walk... Would you mind very much if I walked with you?"

"Be my guest," Boxer replied.

They left the hotel lobby, and as they turned toward the river, Boxer said, "The name Wright is beginning to ring a bell... Something to do with construction." He stopped and snapped his fingers. "The Wright Construction Company."

"You got it," she laughed.

"Your husband —"

"Ex-husband."

Boxer nodded... He remembered having seen the stories in the newspapers. The divorce became a public spectacle, especially since there were photographs of Mr. Wright and some young model frolicking nude in his pool...

"No comments?" she asked.

"None."

"No questions, either?"

"None."

"I think we'll get along fine," she said, suddenly linking her arm with his.

What Boxer realized he didn't need, was another woman. He already had two: one all fire and light, the other all smoke and mystery. But he also knew that what kismet brings, kismet brings, and, if he'd learned anything, he learned never to deny kismet, because it can't be denied. Maybe put off. But never, absolutely never, denied...

CHAPTER 15

Smith sat directly in front of Tosenko's desk. The Russian was a bear of a man, complete with black, bushy eyebrows that joined together. For many years he had been the captain of a fish factory ship that operated in the Antarctic Ocean, and his weather-beaten face was the only visible evidence of that experience. But the years spent in the harshest environment in the world made him uniquely fitted for the position he now held — overall director of the company.

"Boxer and Borodine are going to start a campaign for our respective governments to do something about the dumping of nuclear waste in the North Pacific," Smith said.

"How much do they know?"

"They have the submarine's log, and the results of one or more autopsies," Smith said.

Tosenko said, "I had the submarine blown off its perch."

"Yes, I know you did... Our sensors picked up the explosion, and pinpointed its origin."

Tosenko helped himself to a cigar, and offered one to Smith.

"Cuban cigars are still the best," Smith said, when the two of them were smoking.

"No doubt about that," Tosenko responded. "I always had them aboard the ship... They were one of the few pleasures I had." Then he said, "Hale made a mistake."

Smith nodded.

"Has his death been linked to Negron's?" Tosenko asked.

"Not that I know... But Lillian has been identified," Smith said.

"By whom?"

"Her friend, a freelance writer named Kate Brennan," Smith said.

"Did Hale kill Lillian?"

Smith shrugged. "After it happened, he called me, and said that she went out of the window."

"Did he say why she went out of the window? A person just doesn't jump out of the window from —"

"He was going to turn her over to Miguel," Smith said.

"What a waste..." Tosenko said.

"She certainly knew how to please a man," Smith replied.

Tosenko flicked the ash off the tip of cigar into a cut-glass ashtray. "I can certainly block Borodine's report from getting anywhere near the top people, and I suspect you can do the same thing."

"I can do it, but Boxer will certainly try other avenues."

"Meaning, of course, he'll use his influence to bring the message to the people, and force your government to make some sort of a response?"

"In a word, yes."

Tosenko ran his fingers through his hair, then he said, "We'll have to wait and see what happens. If either Boxer or Borodine becomes too much of a problem, then we'll have to take whatever steps are necessary to eliminate the problem."

"Don't think in terms of buying them off," Smith said. "Boxer was a multimillionaire before the salvage, now he's some twenty million dollars richer, as is Borodine. And Stark's money will eventually go to Boxer."

"Who is Stark?"

"A retired CNO, and Boxer's surrogate father."

"Then Stark will be the way we will, if necessary, get to Boxer," Tosenko said.

"I don't like that."

"Can you think of a better idea?"

"Why not Borodine's family?" Smith said.

"Certainly, why not?"

Smith took a deep drag on the cigar, and held the smoke for a few moments, before he let it rush out of his nose and mouth. "I will be at the Russian Embassy tonight. If I find out anything interesting, I'll let you know."

Tosenko nodded and said, "If it's possible to do it without arousing questions, I want you to claim Lillian's body."

Smith raised his eyebrows questioningly.

"I wouldn't want to think of her in a pauper's grave," he said. "For the pleasure she gave me, I feel I can give her something in return."

Smith nodded... *Hard as the man is, he actually had feelings for the woman...*

"Our business is done?" Tosenko asked.

"All except the question of what I should do with Lillian's body, if I should be able to get it?"

"Have it cremated, and send the ashes to me," Tosenko said. "I'll dispose of them."

The two men stood up and shook hands.

Boxer and Mrs. Wright walked along the Potomac. She told him that she'd much prefer to be called Connie, rather than Constance, or Mrs. Wright, which sounded much too formal.

Boxer didn't tell her much about himself, and she was just as unwilling to talk about herself. She seemed to want to be with him for company, nothing more. And that suited Boxer.

By the time they returned to the hotel, the afternoon was beginning to fade into the autumnal twilight. And it was colder.

They rode up the elevator together, and when they reached their floor and left it, Connie said, "Thank you, Jack, for a lovely walk."

"And thank you," he said, "for the same lovely walk."

She laughed. "Perhaps we might do it again sometime?"

"I'd like that."

"Call me when you want my company," she said.

"I will," Boxer said.

She leaned close, kissed his cheek, then turned, and went to her suite.

Moments later, he was inside his, and the phone was ringing. He picked it up.

Stark was on the other end.

"How are you feeling?" Boxer asked.

"Lousy... But I'll feel much better the moment I get out of here," Stark said in his gravelly voice. "You coming down for the weekend?"

"Yes... I might have a friend with me," Boxer said.

"If you can bear it, so can I," Stark answered.

"I'll stop on the way down and do some shopping," Boxer told him.

"I'm getting out of here early tomorrow morning, and I've made arrangements to have a limo drive me down."

"All right, I'll see you Friday evening," Boxer said.

"See you," Stark answered and clicked off.

Boxer put the phone down and smiled... He loved that cranky old man...

Boxer saw Kate enter the hotel lobby. He'd just left the elevator car.

She saw him, broke into a smile, and running across the lobby, flung herself into his arms.

143

Boxer kissed her passionately. "My God, it's good to hold you," he told her, pressing her even more fiercely against himself.

"It's good to have you hold me," Kate answered.

He could smell the delicious scent of her perfume.

"I think people are looking at us," she told him.

"Do you care?"

"Not in the least."

Boxer kissed her again, and this time, before he let her go, he said, "Why don't we go upstairs and finish what we started down here?"

She laughed and answered, "Because that's for later, my love... Now, I am going to take you to dinner."

"What's this thing you suddenly developed about having dinner?" Boxer asked, and as they started toward the lobby door, he saw Connie. She was standing off to the left, looking daggers at him and Kate. Obviously, she'd witnessed their emotional greeting.

"And who is *she*?" Kate whispered.

"Someone I just met this afternoon. She has a suite on the same floor as mine," he explained.

"She's staked you out for herself," Kate said.

They left the lobby.

"You didn't answer my question," Boxer said, wanting to switch the subject.

"My car is up the street," Kate told him, then linking her arm with his, she added, "I'll scratch her eyes out, if she comes near you."

"Kate!"

"Listen, I not only enjoy sleeping with you, I actually enjoy *being* with you!"

"I appreciate the compliment, but I don't know the woman — that is to say, I just met her."

"And I'll scratch your eyes out, if I find out that you're trying to get to know her."

"Kate!" he exclaimed again.

She stopped suddenly, faced him, and putting her arms around him, she pressed herself against him. "That's me," she said, in a low, passionate voice, "and that me is yours."

Boxer kissed her, and at the same time caressed the side of her face with his hand.

"Good, I'm glad we understand one another," Kate said, when they separated.

"Now, are you going to tell me about dinner?" Boxer asked.

"Not a word," she answered.

They reached the car, she beeped the alarm off, opened the door on the driver's side, then, reaching over, she unlocked the door for Boxer.

"While you were away, the newspapers ran a story about your salvage operation," Kate said, a few moments after they pulled away from the curb.

"Anything interesting?"

"Something about everyone who was in on it will have a ton of money, if it was successful."

"A half ton at least," Boxer laughed.

"Those three hardcase types I met — how did they work out?" Kate asked.

"Just fine," Boxer said, moving to look at her from an angle. She was a beautiful woman.

"You're staring at me," she said, glancing at him.

Boxer nodded. "You're absolutely right: I am staring at you."

"You're making me feel self-conscious."

"You, self-conscious? Never happen!"

She laughed. "Well, maybe not."

"Anyone ever tell you they looked good enough to eat?" Boxer asked.

"Some have," she answered. "You, for one … but you're just going to have to wait until sometime after dinner for that, unless you want me to wind the two of us up on top of a telephone pole, or worse, in the hospital?"

The two of them exploded into laughter.

When they had quieted down, Kate said, "We're going to have dinner with Detective Captain Green… I invited him —

"Jack, I want to find out what really happened to Lillian," Kate said. "Green doesn't know you'll be with me."

"You mean he thinks he's going to be alone with you?"

She glanced at him. "Not really alone alone."

"What did you tell him?"

"I've been in touch with him over the last week — since I identified Lillian's body — and I called and told him that to show my appreciation —"

"You sure he doesn't expect you to show something else?"

"Jack, the man has been helpful."

"If he's been helpful, why did you arrange this little get together for us?" Boxer asked, more than annoyed that he'd been used by Kate.

"Because he might —"

"You know, if I didn't love you, I'd get out of the car," Boxer said. "You could have told me straight out who you wanted me to meet and why."

She reached across him, took hold of his hand, brought it back to her thigh, and asked, "Would you have come with me, if I had leveled with you?"

"Probably not," Boxer answered, gently squeezing her thigh. "But don't ever pull something like this again."

"Absolutely not," she said.

"Not until you feel it is necessary," he said sarcastically.

She looked at him and smiled.

"At least tell me where we're going to meet him?" Boxer said.

"At his place. He's a bachelor, and he's cooking dinner."

"And you told me he didn't expect to be alone with you?"

"Isn't it a shame that the best laid plans of mice and men go astray," Kate said.

"We'll be very lucky if he doesn't poison us," Boxer responded.

Kate found Green's house, or more precisely Green's hideaway, obviously a converted barn that had once been part of a farm.

Wearing a chef's hat and a white apron, Green stood in the doorway, eager to greet Kate, and more than surprised when he saw Boxer. But Kate carried off the introductions airily, even before she and Boxer reached the doorway. By the time they did, Green had recovered from the shock of seeing Boxer, and vigorously shook his hand.

"Jack has just returned from salvaging a fortune in gold," mentioned Kate, as Green finished supplying each of them, including himself, with a drink. They settled in the living room, she and Boxer on the sofa, and Green in an easy chair.

"Boxer..." Green said, then snapping his fingers, he mentioned the newspaper article. "I knew the name sounded familiar, but I couldn't place it." He removed the apron, but left the chef's hat on.

"This is a lovely place," Kate commented, twisting around to the right and then the left. "Did you do the renovation?"

Green laughed and shook his head. "I'm all thumbs. No, I had professionals do it. But I'm responsible for everything else."

"The decorating?"

"Yes... Some of the painting and sketches you see on the walls are mine."

"I'm impressed," she said. "I would never have suspected that, as the saying goes, *underneath that tough police exterior is an artist's soul.*"

Green made a broad, open gesture with his hands. "Each one of us are a composite of many different people," he said.

Boxer didn't enter the conversation. Instead, he left the couch and walked around the room, looking at the paintings. Many were of nudes, and they were wonderfully erotic; there were street scenes, and these were almost like photographs. The rest were a mixed bag of landscapes, especially trees and rocks. All of them were, in his opinion, very good. And when he returned to the couch, he said so.

"Now, if you like my cooking as much as you like my paintings, we'll be friends for life," Green laughed.

"I think we'll be friends, even if I don't like your cooking," Boxer said, aware that Green was having a real problem keeping his eyes off Kate's bare thighs, which were barely covered by the bottom of her cocktail dress.

"Was your salvage operation successful?" Green asked, and before Boxer could answer, Kate said, "I know we spoke about it coming out here, but I don't think I ever asked you whether or not it was successful... Was it?"

"Very."

"Then you're even wealthier than you were before," she laughed.

"Yes."

Green uttered a deep sigh, and said, "If I had money enough, I'd say to hell with my pension, quit the force, and devote my time to painting." Then, with a broad smile, he added, "But since that is out of the question, let's deal with the reality of the situation... I made roast leg of lamb for the main course, broiled shrimp in a spicy sauce for an appetizer, and for dessert, blueberry pie with ice cream."

"The pie and ice cream are yours?" Kate asked.

"Only the pie... The ice cream comes from a local place in town. But it's as close to homemade as you can get."

The rest of the evening went quickly, dissolving in time spent eating and talking.

Most of the conversation was between Green and Kate. Boxer marveled at how facile she was at moving from topic to topic. And when dinner was finished, she told their host how delicious the food was.

"It certainly was excellent," Boxer said.

"I'm glad you liked it," Green answered, and suggested they return to the living room for an after dinner drink.

It was then that Kate said, "I brought Jack here, because I asked him to help me find out who killed Lillian."

"I figured as much," Green said, warming his brandy by holding the snifter glass between his hands, and gently rotating it so that the liquid swirled around.

"I don't know why she thinks I can help," Boxer said. "But if you don't mind, I'd like to know what you have on the case so far."

Green nodded. "I don't see any harm in telling you. But I'll warn you not to think of acting on your own... Leave it to the professionals."

Boxer nodded.

"Well, you know about Lillian — she was either thrown or jumped out a window in a penthouse apartment that belonged to a Mr. Hale. She was completely naked. That in itself might not be strange, but the coroner found cigarette burn marks on her breast and face."

"You never mentioned that to me," Kate said in a low, tremulous voice.

Boxer took hold of her hand, and gently squeezed.

"Two days after Lillian went out of the window of his penthouse, Hale was burned alive in a white Mercedes, a few miles outside of Annapolis. We believe the two are connected."

"Anything more than just your belief to go on?" Boxer asked.

Green nodded and said, "The night that Lillian either jumped or was pushed out of the window, another killing took place... A man Lillian had met that same evening, Commander William Negron —"

"Say again," Boxer said, getting to his feet.

"Commander William Negron, he was with the ONI—"

"For Christ sakes, he was a junior officer aboard the *Shark!*" Boxer exclaimed.

"I'm sorry," Green said.

Boxer ran his hand over his chin, sat down, and in a hard voice, he said, "All right, tell me the rest."

"Commander Negron was gunned down in his apartment, at about three-thirty in the morning. Before he returned home, he had used a public phone to make a recording of his meeting with Lillian."

"My God, she told me about him," Kate exclaimed.

"When?" Green asked.

"Before she was killed... She was in her apartment. She called me, and told me she met a man, a naval officer, who she —" Kate's voice suddenly broke, and she began to weep.

Boxer handed her his handkerchief.

"What did she say?" Green asked gently.

"She said, 'I could feel the electricity between us... I know he's going to contact me,'" Kate told them.

Green got up and said, "I could use another brandy... Anyone else want a refill?"

Boxer handed him his glass.

Green walked over to the bar cart, and while he poured the brandy into the glasses, he asked, "Did Lillian tell you anything more about Commander Negron?"

"Only that he was good-looking, and took a lot of shit from Hale."

Green came back to where Boxer and Kate were sitting, gave Boxer his drink, and sitting down, he said, "Commander Negron went to Lillian's apartment that same night, and according to the report he made, she told him that Hale, and most of the men she entertained, were involved in the nuclear power industry in some way... Some of them were foreigners, diplomats, or industrialists."

"How did you come by all of this information?" Boxer asked.

"I went to see the Director of the Office of Naval Intelligence," Green answered. "Commander Negron was investigating Hale."

"Why?"

Green shrugged. "I wasn't told," he said. "It comes under a security blanket."

Boxer nodded. "I'm surprised you were told as much as you were... The NIO is tight-lipped about their agents."

151

"I threatened to get a court order."

"That wouldn't have done it... With all due respect, you were given only as much as they wanted you to know. The tip of the proverbial iceberg."

"Do you think you can find out any more?" Kate asked.

"I sure as hell am going to try... William was a friend of mine."

Green took a sip of his drink, and said, "So now we have three deaths, two definitely murders, and one either a murder or a suicide, but certainly connected to the other two deaths."

"What in hell is someone trying to protect?" Boxer asked, as he stood up and began to pace.

"Maybe you'll find out, Jack, from the ONI," Kate said.

He stopped, looked at her, and suddenly found himself wondering if she could be the fourth victim?

"What's wrong?" she asked.

"We met Hale and Lillian," he said.

"Yes, briefly."

"He knew that you were Lillian's friend, didn't he?"

"Are you suggesting —" she began.

"He's suggesting that Hale could have passed that information on to someone, and that someone might have been responsible for his death and Lillian's, and that your life might now be at risk," Green said.

"Don't be absurd," Kate answered.

Boxer said, "It might be absurd, but it is certainly a possibility."

"What about you?"

"*What about me?*"

"You met him, too. Doesn't that put you at risk? After all, Commander Negron was on your team."

Though she had a point, Boxer wasn't going to concede it. "I'm paid to put my life at risk. You're not."

She gestured toward Green. "In this situation, *he's* the only one paid to put his life at risk?

"Negron was one —"

"Don't give me that old saw... *He was one of my men etcetera etcetera*, because I'm not going to buy it."

Rubbing his hand across his jaw, Boxer said, "I don't want you to wind up the way Lillian did."

"Listen to him," Green told her.

"Stay at my place, stay here — I'm sure you'll be welcome — but don't stay in your own apartment, at least not for a while."

"You really think I might be in danger?" Kate asked, much of the bravado now gone.

"The operating word is *might*, which makes it conditional," Green explained, and then he added, "You are really welcome to stay here."

"Jack?" Kate said.

"My place until —"

"Yes?" she asked.

"I have just the place ... with Stark."

"That old man who went with you?"

"That 'old man' is —" He stopped again. "Doesn't matter what he is to me. You'll be safe with him. He has a house down on the coast, a few hours' drive from Washington. I was going to take you down there this weekend, anyway."

"Well, I'm glad we got that settled," Green said. "For a few moments there, I was afraid that I'd have to referee an argument, or maybe be asked to arbitrate."

Boxer sat down again and, taking hold of Kate's hand said, "I might argue with her, but it would be impossible for me to be angry with her for very long."

Green nodded. "I can understand that."

Boxer knew he could... If ever a man's yearning for a woman showed in his eyes, it showed in Green's...

"I could use another drink," Kate announced.

"Yes, I could, too," Green said. "What about you, Jack?"

"I'll pass... I'm sure I'll be driving back to the city," Boxer answered.

Hours later, Boxer and Kate lay naked in his bed.

He kissed her gently on the tip of her nose and putting his arm around her, he drew her to him.

"You know Green surprised me," she said after a while. "I didn't know he painted, or was anything like he was."

"The man has a bad case of the hots for you," Boxer said.

"Not because I gave him any reason to," she answered.

Boxer laughed. "You're the reason... You're *one hell of a sexy-looking broad.*"

"Is that all you think I am: a *sexy-looking broad*, as you just said?"

"A very brainy one."

"You can do better than that," she challenged, resting her head on her hand.

"You want the bottom line?"

"The absolute bottom," she responded.

"All right. But just remember, you asked for it," he told her. She nodded.

"You're *a brainy, sexy-looking broad*, who also happens to have a wonderful bottom and is an extraordinary lay."

"All that?"

"How much more complimentary do you want me to be?" Boxer asked.

"Well..."

"Okay, there's one more thing."

"Yes?"

"You smell great," Boxer said.

"I smell great?"

Boxer nodded.

"Describe it."

He thought for a moment, then he said, "Animal-like... Sexy animal-like."

She repeated what he'd just said, and added, "I'll have to think about it."

"You do that," Boxer said, drawing her face close to his and kissing her on the lips. "It's way past my bedtime."

"Do you want me to tell you what I think you are?" she asked.

"No. I want to go to sleep," Boxer said.

"Good. I'm glad you want to hear."

"I'm not going to have much choice in the matter," he said.

"None... You're a self-assured, sexually adept man, who knows how to satisfy women in various ways, who is also highly intelligent, and who is utterly impossible!"

Boxer laughed and said, "I am more than possible, my love... I am me... Now, let's get some sleep."

"After."

"After what?" he asked.

"After you make love to me," she said.

"How did I know that was coming?"

She shrugged and said, "Because you're you."

The two of them guffawed...

As it usually did, the reception at the Russian Embassy lasted into the early hours of the next day. And Smith had made it a point to spend time with Borodine, who much to his surprise was toasted by the Russian Ambassador and several other embassy officials for his part in the salvage operation, and his "fearless examination of one of our submarines." Then it was Dr. Ioff's turn to be toasted "for her dedication to the profession."

Over vodka and caviar, Smith told Borodine that he was in "total sympathy with any movement that would stop the illegal dumping of waste in the ocean, regardless of what the waste is."

"I'm very glad to hear that, Mister Secretary," Borodine said, "because neither I nor Admiral Boxer want to become involved in an argument with members of our respective governments... To us, there isn't even an issue. It is wrong; therefore, it must be stopped." Then raising his vodka glass, he said, "To clean oceans!"

Smith clinked his glass against Borodine's, and responded, "That's certainly worth drinking to."

After they drank, Smith said, "I'd like very much to be introduced to Dr. Ioff... Perhaps she'd be willing to speak to some members of the staff at the Bethesda Naval Hospital?"

"That's something you'll have to take up with her," Borodine said. "But I will introduce you. Come, she's with my wife, near the door."

Smith nodded. "You lead and I'll follow."

Borodine threaded his way through the crowded room, stopping now and then to acknowledge a compliment from a well-wisher, or greet a friend.

Finally, they reached the two women. Borodine introduced his wife and Ilia to Smith, who greeted each of them by vigorously shaking their hands.

"If you will excuse us," Borodine said, placing his hand on his wife's arm, "there are some comrades I would like to see."

Both Smith and Ilia nodded, and when they were alone, Smith said, "I was very impressed with what I heard about you tonight."

She flushed. "Mister Secretary —"

"If we dispense with the titles, it will make it easier for us to speak to one another," Smith said. He was becoming increasingly aware of just how attractive she was. "My given name is William, but all of my friends call me Bill."

"Ilia," she said.

He repeated the name, looked straight at her, and said, "It fits."

She flushed again.

"I'd like to know more about your experiences aboard the SSN-S1," he said. "I think you're the first Russian doctor to serve aboard an American naval vessel."

"There should be an exchange program in place," Ilia said. "That way both sides would benefit."

"Yes, that would certainly be useful," he said, and taking hold of her hand, he asked, "May I offer you something to eat and drink? There's an enormous buffet."

She laughed and nodded.

Smith escorted her to the buffet, and together they moved down its length, choosing whatever food caught their fancy.

"I'll never eat everything on this plate," Ilia said, as they sat down at an empty table.

Smith laughed. "I don't think I will either, but everything looked so very good." Then he said, "I think we should pursue the idea of exchanging naval medical teams."

"We?"

"Certainly 'we,'" he said. "It was your idea... Besides, it will give me a reason to see you again, not that I really need another one."

"Mister— "

He waved a finger at her. "Informal. Remember?"

"Bill, I'd rather not have you thinking —"

He threw up his hands. "Friends, then... Just friends."

"Friends," she repeated with a smile.

"Now tell me about the radiation you encountered?" he asked, spearing a steaming piece of kielbasa with his fork.

"It was a thousand times stronger that what is considered a normal dosage," she said. "The men aboard the boat died of acute radiation sickness. Their red blood cells were destroyed. Borodine and the rescue team brought back two bodies. They are aboard the SSN-S1."

Smith shook his head, and in a sympathetic tone, he said, "It must have been terrible for those men."

"In the end they lacked the strength to operate the boat," she said, then added, "Comrade Admiral Borodine and other members of his team actually went inside. He can give you more details about how he found them."

"Then Admiral Boxer didn't go?"

"No. He commanded the entire operation from the CR — I'm sorry — the Control Room of the SSN-S1," Ilia answered.

"I find that extraordinarily interesting," Smith commented.

Ilia laughed. "Admiral Boxer is an extraordinary man."

"Yes, I'm beginning to believe that, especially, if a woman like you says that he is," Smith responded, aware, now, of where her romantic interests were.

She missed his innuendo, and said, "He doesn't know what fear is, and makes almost impossible demands on himself to meet the needs of his command."

"We need more men like him," Smith said, wondering if she had any idea of Boxer's many, many love affairs?

"His men idolize him," Ilia continued.

"Yes, I have been told that they did," Smith answered, and then to get her off the subject of Boxer, he suggested they go to the bar.

"I'll go with you, but I'm not much of a drinker," she said. "I don't seem to tolerate it well, and I don't like what it does to me." She laughed. "It brings out the darker side of my nature."

"Forgive me, if I say that *sounds exciting.*"

"It's not. It's ugly," Ilia said with conviction.

"Coffee, then?" he suggested.

"No, I'll go to the bar with you. There's no reason why you should deny yourself, because of me." Getting to her feet, she reached down, took hold of his hand, and gently pulled him up.

Smith let her lead him to the bar... Not only had he learned about her two weaknesses, but he had also learned about the two bodies aboard the SSN-S1, and that, in the immediate future, was more important than knowing that Ilia was in love with Boxer, and that alcohol probably changed her personality...

CHAPTER 16

During the next few days, Boxer worked on his report, alternately dated Kate and Ilia, and though he very much wanted to become intimate with the beautiful doctor, she always managed to avoid it. Once she told him, "It's not that I don't want to sleep with you, it's that I do not want to carry the extra burden that it would give me…"

Boxer, a patient man when involved with a woman, did not press the matter. He was, for the first time, emotionally involved with two different women, and he knew that if he were asked which of the two he loved, he'd have to answer, *both*.

He took Kate down to Stark's place early Friday, knowing that the SSN-S1 was due sometime after midnight Saturday. Borodine had volunteered to go down to Norfolk, and supervise the unloading of the gold. He also had to make the necessary arrangements to have the bodies of the Russian submariners sent to the Navy Medical Laboratories in Bethesda.

Stark proved to be in rare form, and he and Kate hit it off immediately. In the evening, as the three of them sat on the deck and looked out at the gathering darkness over the ocean, Stark announced, "If you don't marry this woman, Jack, I will."

"Is that a proposal, Admiral?" Kate asked.

"It's as close as you're going to get to one from me," Stark said in his gravelly voice.

Kate took hold of his hand and said, "In that case, I'll accept… Being married to you, Admiral, with all due respect, would be a hell of a lot less exhausting than being married to Jack."

Boxer kept a straight face, though he wanted desperately to laugh.

Stark squinted at her. "Are you telling me something, young lady?" he questioned.

She let go of his hand, and fluttering her eyelashes at him, she said, "Why, Admiral, whatever gave you that idea?"

Stark studied her for a moment, then broke up with laughter, and that was the signal for Boxer and Kate to laugh, too.

When it became too dark for them to see the ocean, they went to the Chowder House for dinner, where Stark and Boxer got a rousing welcome from the owners and locals.

Later, when Boxer and Kate were in bed, she said, "I had a wonderful time. I like this place, and I like the Admiral."

"He likes you, too," Boxer answered.

She laughed and said, "The two of you are so much alike, it's absolutely uncanny."

"He's more crotchety than I am."

"Oh, you have your moments," she told him.

"But this doesn't happen to be one of them," he said, taking her in his arms and kissing her passionately.

"I didn't think it was," Kate answered.

Boxer slept soundly, until the shrill ring of the telephone began to slash at him. Finally, he answered it.

Sarkis was on the other end.

Boxer looked at the digital clock on the night table. It's red numbers showed 04:10:25. Except for the glow of the numbers, the room was very dark, and cold.

"Admiral?" Sarkis questioned.

"I'm here," Boxer answered.

161

Kate stirred and pulled herself up.

"Sir, the bodies of the Russian sailors are gone," Sarkis said.

Boxer sat up. "Gone? Gone where?"

"There was a van on the pier —"

"You mean that there was someone there to pick up those bodies?"

"Yes, sir... And they had the necessary ID and papers," Sarkis said.

"Where is Comrade Admiral Borodine?" Boxer asked.

"On his way from the motel... Something happened to his car."

"Exactly what happened to his car?"

"I don't know, sir... But he couldn't drive it," Sarkis answered.

"Secure the boat, no one is to be allowed on or off, unless he's a member of the crew... Inform Comrade Admiral Borodine of my orders, and about the men who picked up the bodies of the Russian sailors. Use our men to unload the gold."

"Aye, aye, sir," Sarkis answered.

"Next time, Commander, if you have any doubts about doing something, don't wait until *after* you do it to call your superior officer."

"Yes, sir."

"I'll be down there sometime later today," Boxer said.

"Yes, sir," Sarkis answered, then he asked, "Sir, do you want Comrade Admiral Borodine to call you?"

"No need for him to do that," Boxer answered grumpily, and slammed the phone down.

"What was that all about?" Kate asked.

"The opening salvo of the war between the good guys and the bad guys," he answered.

"It's cold out here... Come on under the blanket and tell me about it," Kate said, sliding herself down again.

Boxer joined her.

"Are you going to tell me?" she said.

"Do you remember that Russian submarine that went down in the Arctic?"

"Yes... It was on the news for a couple of nights."

"We answered their mayday, but we were too late," Boxer said.

"That was never in the news," she said.

Boxer shrugged. "Igor went inside. The entire crew was dead... They had all died from acute radiation sickness... Igor recovered the boat's log, and brought two bodies back to our boat."

"Those are the bodies that are missing?"

"Yes."

"And the log?"

"Still on board," Boxer answered.

Kate emitted a long, low whistle, then she asked, "Does the log give any indication of what happened?"

"There's a place in the North Pacific that they just happened to get too close to, that apparently is being used to dump nuclear waste material."

Almost simultaneously the two of them bolted up.

"Are you thinking what I am thinking?" Kate asked.

"That's what Lillian had mentioned to Negron," Boxer said. "Almost all of the men she entertained had something to do with nuclear waste."

Kate switched on the light. "I won't be able to sleep," she said, leaving the bed and putting on a white terry cloth robe.

Boxer got out of bed and put on his black jogging suit.

"I'll go down to the kitchen and make us a pot of coffee," Kate said.

Boxer nodded, and following her out of the bedroom, he said, "I'm going to leave for Norfolk in a couple of hours."

"I want to go with you," Kate said, as she measured out the coffee for the automatic coffeemaker.

"No way... Whoever is running the operation is a hardball player... I want you here safe."

"It's a big story, Jack, and I want it before anyone else begins to sniff around its edges," Kate said, as she poured coffee into two different mugs.

"I promise you'll get it," Boxer said, picking up one of the mugs. "But I want you alive."

"Jack, I won't stay here!"

He looked at her over the rim of the mug. No matter what he'd tell her, she still would do what she wanted, especially if she could get a good story out of it...

He lowered the mug, and said, "All right, you can go, but not with me. Go to Green and tell him about the two bodies, and what I just told you. See if he doesn't make the same connection that we did."

"He must."

"There isn't any *must*," Boxer said. "But if he does, tell him to start looking for those bodies... We need them to convince the various governments to take action now and destroy that dump site."

She grinned at him, put her mug down, and putting her arms around his neck, she said, "I love you, Jack Boxer."

"I want you back here by evening," Boxer said.

"I promise," Kate answered, pressing her body against his.

"You're a hussy, do you know that? Don't answer," he said, and sweeping her up into his arms, he carried her upstairs...

"Someone took my distributor cap," Borodine said, "and at that hour, I couldn't rent another car."

"Well, let's hope Green can find the bodies," Boxer responded. "But the way they're shielded, it won't be easy."

Borodine didn't answer.

The two of them were standing on the foredeck of the SSN-S1, a brisk wind was blowing off the James River, and the sky was filled with mares' tails.

"I think that tug is for us," Borodine said, gesturing to the boat, moving slowly toward them.

"Did the yard officer give you any indication of how long it would take to replace the drive shaft, and weld in new plates on the outer hull?" Boxer asked.

"Two weeks, at the most, working regular shifts."

"Do you have his phone number?"

"Yes."

Boxer smiled and said, "*This is Admiral Hays. I want that work done on the SSN-S1 done in a week.*"

"You wouldn't dare do that," Borodine said with a smile.

"*Yes, I'll see the paperwork down, authorizing the overtime,*" Boxer said, continuing with the accent.

"But why would you —"

"Listen," Boxer said, "those little twitches I get down my spine when I sense something is going wrong, well, I'm getting them now."

"Jack, that's putting yourself in jeopardy!"

"First, I'm going below to make that phone call before the phone lines are disconnected, and the tug takes her in tow. Then I'll tell you about a couple of murders that might have some connection to that hot zone in the North Pacific," Boxer said.

Within minutes, Boxer and Borodine were below in Boxer's cabin, and Boxer was on the phone with the yard officer, Captain Charles Brody.

"I must have the papers, Admiral," Brody said. "This means making a shift in my workforce."

Boxer put his hand on the mouthpiece, and said, "Brody wants the papers."

"So would I, if I were him."

"You start the work today, and I promise you that by tomorrow, I will give you a letter giving you the authorization to change your work schedule." Boxer continued the impersonation.

"What about the cost breakdown? This means overtime for the workers."

"When I have the letter delivered, you give me Xerox copies of the present cost schedule, and I'll have the new one in your hands by the next day."

"That will be two and half days into the work," Brody said.

"Captain, a little accommodation would be much appreciated," Boxer told him.

"Well, sir, it's not that I want to be a stickler for the regs, but we're talking about an expenditure of several millions of dollars."

"I certainly appreciate your concern for the way the Navy spends its money, Captain, and I certainly will remember this *favor*, and if I can reciprocate in the future in any way, please call me."

"Yes, sir," Brody answered.

Boxer thanked him again, and put down the phone.

"And just how are you going to manage to get Admiral Hays to write the letter?" Borodine asked.

"He won't, but I will."

Borodine threw his hands up into the air.

"I'll handle this. It has nothing to do with you," Boxer said.

Suddenly, 1MC came on, and the WO announced that the boat was going to be taken in tow within thirty minutes.

"Let's go out to that diner outside the main gate," Boxer said. "I haven't had breakfast yet."

"Neither have I," Borodine said.

The two left the boat, and drove their respective cars to the diner, where they sat down in a booth next to a window.

Before the waitress came to take their orders, Boxer told Borodine about how Lillian died, then Negron, and finally Hale. "Hale was involved with people in the nuclear business here, in your country, and in other countries. At least, that's what she told Negron."

"Let me see if I understand this," Borodine said. "Hale had Lillian and Negron killed, because she told Negron about his connection to the nuclear waste disposal —"

"I didn't say anything about nuclear waste disposal," Boxer said.

"All right, then — the nuclear business."

Boxer nodded.

"You're assuming that Lillian's death and Negron's stem from that?"

"Yes."

"And that Hale had ordered the two of them killed."

"Probably."

"Then why was Hale killed?"

Boxer shrugged.

"You're also assuming that the people responsible for Hale's death are responsible for creating the hot zone, and stealing the two bodies?"

"Yes."

"And you're saying that someone other than the members of the crew knew about the bodies?"

"Someone who is also connected to the people who are responsible for the three killings," Boxer said.

Borodine leaned back. "You are doing a lot of assuming in order to get where you are," he said.

"That's all I can do now," Boxer said.

"You still haven't told me *why* you want the SSN-S1 to be repaired so quickly," Borodine responded.

Boxer smiled. "Because we might have to use it, Igor."

"Steal it?"

"Borrow it for a while," Boxer said.

"The hot zone…"

"Those twitches tell me that we're not going to get anywhere with our reports," Boxer said. "And the situation is critical. If we wait —"

"That's piracy!" Borodine exclaimed.

"You're letting your imagination run away with you, Igor," Boxer said.

"And I would have to say that yours has already gone," Borodine responded.

The waitress came to the table. "Are you gentlemen ready — " Her eyes went wide, and she exclaimed, "Oh no!"

Boxer pulled back.

The next instant the window shattered, and she fell backwards. Instantly people began to scream.

Boxer and Borodine were on their feet, and bending over the stricken woman.

"Get an ambulance!" Borodine shouted. The woman had been hit just above her left breast, and was bleeding profusely. He put his coat over her.

Boxer stood up and looked out of the shattered window. No one was in the parking area... Whoever fired the shot, had aimed for him, but he'd moved back an instant before the window shattered... He bent over the woman, and gently stroking her head, he asked what her name was.

"Angie Mannan," she said.

"Angie, you're going to be all right," he assured her. "You will be absolutely all right."

"What am I going to do about my kids?" she whimpered.

"I promise you, they'll be taken care of," Boxer said.

Suddenly the wail of sirens grew louder and louder, and then stopped. Moments later two policemen rushed into the diner.

Boxer and Borodine introduced themselves, and showed the officers their respective ID's.

"We'll need statements from each of you," one of the cops said.

"No problem," Boxer answered. "As soon as we make sure that the woman is taken care of, we'll give you our statements."

The officer nodded.

"I'll ride in the ambulance with her," Boxer said.

Once again the wail of sirens grew louder, then ceased altogether.

"The ambulance is here," someone said.

Within minutes, Angie was loaded into the back of the ambulance, and Boxer and Borodine were seated on a bench opposite her.

"I guess your assumptions are pretty good ones," Borodine said, as the sirens began to wail again, and they began to move.

Boxer nodded.

"My kids are in school," Angie said.

"We'll get them, and bring them to the hospital for you."

"What about my job? What about —"

Boxer put his finger over her lips. "Angie, trust me... You might not think so now, but this is the luckiest day of your life." He had already decided to provide a substantial amount of money for her and her children. There wasn't any doubt that she took the bullet that was meant for him...

CHAPTER 17

When Boxer and Borodine turned in their reports, each was told — though not in the same words, but essentially the same meaning — *Very good work, but don't hold your breath until you hear from us.* And to add to their frustrations, Green wasn't able to find the slightest trace of the missing bodies.

And for Boxer the feeling of frustration was increased, because Ilia was too busy to see him. When Borodine mentioned that "your Secretary of the Navy has been seeing a lot of her," Boxer was too surprised to be angry. Besides, his relationship with Kate had really become intense.

He spent a great deal of time with her at Stark's place, while she was putting the finishing touches on the article she was writing for the *Times* Sunday Magazine Section about the hot zone, and its effect on the Russian submarine and the oceans of the world.

Boxer supplied her with all the necessary information, including excerpts from the log of the Russian submarine, translated by Borodine. She even had photographs of the boat's interior, showing the dead Russian sailors. And she dealt with the possibility "that the recent bizarre deaths of a call girl, a naval officer working under cover, and a well-known businessman, appear to have links to the same group who tried to have Admiral Jack Boxer killed, because he has written a report that calls for the governments of the world to destroy the hot zone, and make sure that new hot zones can not be created."

Kate finished the article on Sunday afternoon, and she, Boxer, and Stark celebrated at the Chowder House with a hearty dinner, and two bottles of delicious white wine.

Later, Boxer made love to her, and just before they fell asleep, he said, "You're not only damn good in the sack, you're even better at the typewriter."

"You should see me at a word processor," she answered, snuggling up to him.

"I'll take it to the post office for you, first thing in the morning," Boxer said.

She made an unintelligible sound, that Boxer took for a *yes*, then she was asleep.

Boxer remained awake for a short time longer, and thought about asking Kate to marry him. He enjoyed her company, but was afraid that marriage might spoil the relationship, as it had done for some of his friends. He was also concerned that something as binding as marriage might destroy her spontaneity. And before he could think of anything else, he knew he was drifting off to sleep...

Suddenly, Boxer realized that Kate wasn't in bed. He bolted up. Sunlight filled the room, and the scent of freshly made coffee filled his nostrils.

He put on his skivvies, a bathrobe with a monk's hood, which he did not wear, and a pair of slippers. Then he padded downstairs to the kitchen, expecting to find Kate, instead Stark greeted him with, "You missed her by fifteen minutes... She's on her way to New York. Said she'd be back early this evening."

Boxer's jaw went slack, and before he could recover, the phone rang.

Stark answered it, and as he listened, he began to tremble.

Boxer took the phone from him, and identified himself.

"This is State Police Sergeant Grant of the Highway Patrol, there has been an accident involving your car, Admiral," the voice on the other end said.

"The driver…"

"I'm sorry to have to tell you that the woman driving the car didn't survive."

Boxer swallowed hard, and had to clear his throat several times before he was able to ask, "Do you want me to identify her?"

"Yes, sir… I'll meet you at the local hospital," the trooper said.

"I'll be there in a half hour," Boxer answered, and put the phone down.

With tears streaming down his eyes, Stark said, "I'm going, too."

Boxer nodded. "Take the carbon of her article, when we're finished at the hospital, we're going to New York."

"The best we can figure," Sergeant Grant said, "is that two of her tires were blown out, probably by rifle fire; then the car was fire-bombed… Ms. Brennan never had a chance."

Boxer and Stark walked alongside the trooper, as he led the two of them to the hospital morgue, where Dr. Raji, the hospital's chief pathologist took over, and said, "The body was badly burned."

Boxer nodded.

The doctor looked at Stark.

"I have seen badly burned bodies before, doctor," Stark said in his gravelly voice.

The doctor went to one of the doors in the huge refrigerator, opened it, pulled out the sheet-covered corpse, and quickly lifted the sheet off of the cadaver's head.

Boxer gasped, and Stark uttered a loud groan... Her face was charred, and all of her hair had been burnt off, leaving bits of blackened skin and patches of gray bone visible.

"Thank you," Boxer rasped.

The doctor replaced the sheet, and slid the body back into its refrigerated cubicle.

Boxer cleared his throat. "I will take care of the funeral arrangements."

Dr. Raji nodded.

"Do you know if she has any relatives?" Grant asked.

Boxer shrugged. He'd been living with the woman, and had actually considered marrying her, but he knew practically nothing about her.

"Naturally, they'll have first claim on the body," Grant said.

"We understand," Stark responded, and putting his hand on Boxer's shoulder, he said in low voice, "Let's go Jack... We have something to deliver."

Boxer uttered a ragged sigh, turned, and with Stark alongside, he led the way out of the morgue.

Hours later, after the carbon of Kate's article had been handed over to Mr. Paul Denas, the senior editor of the *Times* Magazine Section, and Boxer had told him how Kate had been killed, and had given him enough material for a follow-up story, Boxer and Stark wound up in the cocktail lounge of St. Regis Hotel.

The two sat opposite each other in a booth, and each nursed a double vodka on the rocks.

"I guess we'll go back tomorrow," Stark said.

"I've already reserved a suite for us," Boxer told him.

Stark raised his eyebrows.

"When you went to the bathroom," Boxer said.

"What else did you do?"

Boxer picked up his glass, and downed the rest of the vodka before he said, "It's not what I've done that matters, it's what I'm going to do."

"I'm listening," Stark told him.

"Nothing is going to be done about the hot zone," Boxer said. "The people who are responsible for it are very high up in government, or they're protected by people who are high up."

"And you're going to bring them down?" Stark questioned, before he finished his drink.

Boxer placed his palms against the edge of the table and pressed hard. "I'm going to destroy them... I'm going to blow them away... That much I owe Kate and the men on the Russian boat..."

"Tell me how."

Boxer relaxed and removed his hands from the edge of the table. "The less you know, the better off you will be."

Stark looked around for their waitress, got her attention, and when she came to the table, he asked for "Two more of the same, and bring something for us to munch on."

"You're going to remain here, until it's done," Boxer said, the moment they were alone again.

"*What?*" Stark said, loud enough for the people at nearby tables to look in his direction.

"I don't want anything to happen to you, because of me," Boxer said. "I want you safe."

"If you want me safe, then —"

"Look, I'm not even sure that I'll be able to do it," Boxer said.

"Tell me how you intend to do it, and maybe I can give you some valuable input."

Boxer thought about that for a few moments, then he said, "Use the SSN-S1 to blow it."

Stark shouted, "What?" and at the same time started to get to his feet.

Boxer motioned him down, and said, "Stop yelling, or we'll be asked to leave."

Stark sat. "And just how are you going to accomplish *that*?"

"Before I answer, I want you to promise you won't shout, jump up, or do anything untoward," Boxer said.

"I have the very definite feeling that I'm not going to like what I hear."

"Promise, or you won't hear anything," Boxer said.

Stark was about to speak, when Boxer bobbed his head to indicate that the waitress was returning.

She set the drinks down, and a bowl of bar nuts.

Stark thanked her, and when she left the table, he said, "All right, you have my word."

"I'm going to steal the boat," Boxer said.

Stark did a double take, then asked, "And just how do you intend to do that when it's being repaired?"

"It will be finished by next Friday," Boxer said.

"How do you know that?"

"Because I anticipated having to do something drastic," Boxer said. "And don't ask what I did, or didn't do, to have it repaired."

Stark shook his head, gulped part of his drink, and asked, "What will you do for a crew?"

"I don't need a full crew... She's sufficiently automated to operate with a dozen men."

"That would be stretching it. But I suppose it could be done."

"Any more questions?"

"Dozens, but I'll only ask one… How do you intend to get close enough to destroy the hot zone?"

"We won't go anywhere near it; that is to say, not within ten miles. We'll send two electronically controlled minisubs in. They'll be loaded with explosives."

"Your plan is to bury the nuclear waste?"

"That's my plan," Boxer responded. "Whatever is there, will be buried under a few million tons of rocks."

Stark finished his drink, then said, "I'm going with you."

Boxer shook his head, "No way… You're not even going to go home, at least not until the hot zone is destroyed… You're going to stay here, in New York, at this hotel, or one of your own choosing. But you not going home."

"Right, I'm not going home… I'm going with you."

"Stark!"

"I'm an old man, but I loved Kate," he said.

Boxer nodded, lifted his drink, and toasted, "To Kate!"

"To Kate!" Stark echoed, touching his glass to Boxer's.

Boxer ate a few bar nuts, before he said, "Borodine won't be with us… He has a family, and I don't want to put them in jeopardy."

"Who'll be your XO?" Stark asked.

"You."

"I thought you didn't want me?"

"I don't, but now that you're coming, I might as well make the best use of you that I can."

"Best use, indeed!" Stark snorted.

"Sarkis, the EO … ten men," Boxer said.

"Have you spoken to them about this yet?"

"I'm meeting with all of them tomorrow."

"Where?"

"Aboard the boat... It will look like a routine meeting, nothing more."

"It would be more routine with Borodine there," Stark said.

Boxer shook his head. "He's out of this one."

"He's not going to like it," Stark said.

"His government would like it a lot more and him a lot less if he came with us."

"What about *your* government? Do you think they're going to take kindly to you stealing one of their submarines?" Stark asked.

"Steal is really the wrong word... I'm going to borrow it," Boxer said.

"I assure you that Admiral Hays — even the President — won't look at it that way."

Boxer shrugged. "Once it's done; it's done."

"Once it's done, you — all of us — could be put away for life," Stark said, finishing his drink.

Boxer rolled his glass between his fingers, then drank the remaining vodka.

"I hope you're not planning to take over Mittenkope's island," Stark said.

Boxer looked at him, and exploded into laughter.

"What the hell is so funny?"

"The thought had occurred to me," Boxer answered, between bursts of laughter; then he said, "Let's go for a walk... I suddenly miss Kate terribly."

Boxer put a twenty-dollar bill down on the table, nodded to Stark, and the two of them left the cocktail lounge, walked across the lobby, and out of the hotel into the cool, quickly gathering twilight of an early November evening.

They were two blocks from the hotel before either one of them spoke, and then Stark said, "Kate looked just like the woman I loved a long time ago... She even had the same name."

"I guessed there was something like that behind your affection for her," Boxer said.

"Something like that," Stark said wistfully. "Something like that..."

CHAPTER 18

All of the men Boxer chose were seated at tables in the wardroom of the SSN-S1. The door was closed, and the vents were closed. He stood near the coffee urn, and said, "I want to destroy the hot zone. To do it, I'm going to have to borrow this boat, and to do that and run, I need you men."

There was a long silence, then the EO said, "When do we go?"

And before Boxer could answer, all of them agreed to join him.

"All right, we go three weeks from tonight, when there will be a new moon," Boxer said. "We need as much cover for the initial stage as we can get. If it rains, or better still, if it snows, we'll be safer.

"Each man will have false orders to take him past the guards at the foot of the pier. Once all of the crew are aboard, we'll slip the boat's lines, backwater until we're in mid-channel, where another submarine — a WWII boat — will be waiting to move into the position occupied by the SSN-S1."

"How can we be sure that the other boat will be there?" Sarkis asked.

"I'll be on it... Once it's in place, I'll go overboard and swim out to where you are."

"A WWII boat doesn't look like —"

"That will be changed... That boat will look exactly like the SSN-S1... But it will be all wood and Styrofoam painted over," Boxer said.

"And where will it come from?" another man asked.

"The Navy is auctioning off several old boats... I'm going to buy one."

"How will you move it here?" Stark asked.

"A tug will bring it."

"A Navy tug?"

Boxer laughed. "With the right kind of papers, you can get anything done."

"Suppose the guards on the pier notice that one boat is moving out, and another one is being moored?" the SO asked.

"That happens all the time," Boxer said. "But just to make sure their suspicions aren't aroused, two things will happen: the COMMO, here, will radio to their booth, ID himself as the yard's security officer, and inform them that SSN-S1 has been ordered to move to Portsmouth, and a new boat, the SSN-24 is being brought in by tug."

"Who'll moor her?"

"Crespo, Zapeda, and Juris. As soon as that's done, they'll walk away. When they get close to the guard house, Zapeda will press an ordinary car alarm switch that will set off two different explosive charges: one aboard the boat they just left, thirty seconds later, one located in a pickup, about fifty yards from the guard house... That will give the guards more than enough to do, and allow our three men to walk away."

"What about supplies?"

"Our three men will meet us at sea eight hours later, and we'll take aboard our supplies; then they'll join us, and we'll destroy the supply barge."

"Then all we have to worry about is the entire United States Navy," the COMMO laughed.

"That's about it," Boxer said. "We'll head for the Arctic, make our way under the ice cap, come out through the Bering Sea, then down to the hot zone."

"Once we blow the hot zone, what will we do?" the DO asked.

"Return to Norfolk."

"What about the guys who'll be out there looking for us?"

"Well, one thing I can guarantee, we won't be looking for them," Boxer said with a straight face.

That brought a burst of laughter from the men.

Then Boxer said, "We're not doing this to have a shootout with the Navy, we're doing it because that hot zone, if not destroyed, will destroy the life in the oceans of the world... We will not make any aggressive move toward any ship, unless that ship fires at us, then we will have no recourse but to return fire. The message will be radioed to Headquarters, as soon as we're ready to dive for the voyage to the hot zone."

"After we take on supplies?" a man asked.

"Yes... Once we dive, we will remain below until we return."

For several moments, no one said anything, then Boxer asked if there were any more questions.

The men were silent.

"Everyone is to be aboard no later than twenty-two hundred... Commander Sarkis will WO, and Admiral Stark will be in command until I come aboard," Boxer told them.

The door and the vents were opened, and the men began to file out.

Later, when Boxer and Stark were driving back to the house on the beach, Stark asked, "Would you really fire on one of our ships?"

"I hope not to have to make that decision," Boxer said. "But if it comes to having to fire to avoid being blown out of the water, I will fire."

A few moments passed, then Stark said, "Sometimes I think you're the hardest man I've ever known, and this is one of those times."

Boxer didn't answer... Sometimes he also thought he was a hard man...

"Stand by to cast off bow and stern lines," Sarkis ordered by radio from the sail's bridge.

There was a quick on-off flash from a flashlight at the bow and the stern.

Sarkis checked the progress of the tug, whose running lights could just be seen through the rain.

"Cast off all lines," he radioed.

This time there were two quick flashes from the bow detail and the stern detail.

Stark came onto the bridge.

"Lines are off, sir," Sarkis reported.

Stark nodded.

"Incoming tide is moving us away from the pier," Sarkis said.

"Slow astern," Stark said.

Sarkis dialed the order in the bridge MCC.

The SSN-S1's propeller began to turn, the boat slowly moved backwards, toward the channel.

"Come to three three five," Stark said.

"Three three five," Sarkis repeated, moving the necessary control dial.

As it backed out into the channel, the stern of the boat began to bear toward the starb'd.

"Tug is beginning to swing toward the pier," Sarkis reported, as he looked through the infrared glasses.

"Give me a distance check to the pier," Stark said.

Sarkis checked the radar display. "Five hundred yards."

"Stop all engines," Stark ordered.

"Stop all engines," Sarkis repeated.

The SSN-S1 continued to move backward, then slowed, and came to a full stop.

Suddenly the radio crackled, and Boxer said, "Stand by to take me aboard on the port side."

"Standing by," Sarkis radioed, then he ordered the two details to take Boxer aboard.

"Tug moving off, boat secured," Stark said, taking his turn and the glasses.

"I'm aboard," Boxer radioed.

"Ahead, one third," Stark ordered.

Sarkis repeated the command, and dialed in the speed.

"Come to new course, two five nine," Stark said.

"New course, two five nine," Sarkis said, making the necessary adjustments.

As the boat gathered headway, and moved into the channel, Boxer came up through the open hatchway onto the bridge. "Smooth as silk, so far," he commented.

"I have our three men in the glasses," Stark said. "They're walking toward the guard house."

"I told them to wait until they're in their getaway car, before they set off the two explosive charges," Boxer said.

"They'll head straight for the supply ship?" Stark asked.

Boxer nodded, and said, "As soon as we hear those explosions, we're going to dive."

"Here?"

"Yes."

"Where's the bottom?"

"Never more than periscope depth, until we clear the bay bridge. I want to run submerged —"

Suddenly two explosions boomed across the water, and where the boat was, a flash of flames burst out of the wet darkness.

Boxer hit the klaxon, then switched on the 1MC. "Dive... Dive... Dive," he ordered.

The men on the bridge went down the open hatchway. Boxer was the last man down. He pulled the hatch shut, dogged it, and went down into the control room, where red light bathed the room.

"Make forty feet," Boxer said.

"Making forty feet," the DO repeated, dialing the value into the master diving control computer.

"UWIS on," Sarkis reported.

"Ahead two-thirds," Boxer ordered.

Sarkis repeated the order, and changed the speed.

"Luckily, there's not much traffic tonight," the SO reported.

Boxer checked the sonar display on the MC. There were two inbound ships, one a tanker, the other, a freighter. The tanker was eight miles away, the freighter eight. Nothing was outward bound.

The SSN-S1 had a clear run to open ocean.

"What are you telling me?" Olsen said, shaking his head.

"The SSN-S1 has been stolen," Hays told him.

Olsen bounced out of his swivel chair.

"It was an almost classic cutting-out operation," Hays said.

"This time Boxer has gone too fucking far out on the limb, and has sawed it off," Olsen fumed.

"You can't be sure it was him."

Olsen whirled around. "As sure as God made little apples," he said.

The door opened, Smith entered. "Is it true?" he asked, gasping for breath. "Did someone steal a submarine?"

"The SSN-S1," Olsen said. "And it wasn't just someone; it was Boxer."

"And what the hell is he going to do with it?" Smith asked, dropping into a chair.

"I suspect he's going to blow the hot zone, as he refers to it," Hays responded.

"Christ!" Smith exclaimed, starting out of his chair.

The phone suddenly rang.

Olsen answered it, listened, and said, "Yes, Mister President... Certainly, they're here in my office, and we will be at your office — A radio message, now... Yes, I will call you back." Olsen put the phone down, reached under the desktop, and pressed a button. A panel on the opposite wall opened, revealing a high-tech communications setup. "Boxer is sending a radio message," Olsen said.

Suddenly, Boxer's voice filled the room... "To the people of the world, this is Admiral Jack Boxer aboard the American submarine SSN-S1... My crew and I have taken over this submarine in order to destroy a hot zone — a place created by unscrupulous men, who are involved in the disposal of nuclear waste. If this is not stopped, the oceans of the world will be contaminated, and your lives and the life of the oceans will be at risk. This can not be allowed to happen. Once we succeed in destroying the hot zone, we will return, and demand that those accountable for the death of an entire crew of a Russian submarine be tried and punished.

"One last word, if we are fired upon, we will defend ourselves. It is not our purpose to seek hostile action, but to those who would try to stop us, I have only one word of advice: Don't."

The phone began to ring again.

"Yes, Mister President, Admiral Boxer told us about the existence of the hot zone," Olsen said. "No, sir, I know nothing about a newspaper article."

"Yes, sir... We are on our way."

Tosenko fumed, "How stupid can your people be, to allow Boxer to steal a submarine?"

Smith shifted his position, and said, "That's not the issue... Now, he has to be stopped. I left the meeting with the President under the pretense of having a sudden, very severe migraine. The United States will not stop Boxer."

"But he stole a submarine!"

Smith ignored what the Russian had just said, and told him, "Your Navy must stop him."

"Orders have already gone out," Tosenko said. "But he belongs to you, and you should be taking care of him."

Smith left his chair. "Was it necessary to kill Kate Brennan?"

"She would have caused even more trouble than she already had," Tosenko answered. "Don't worry, Boxer will not come back to avenge her killing."

Smith shrugged.

"Just how serious are you about Comrade Doctor Ioff?" Tosenko asked.

"I could become *very serious*, but —"

"Another man?"

"Boxer."

Tosenko laughed. "He's out of that picture, and he's out of every other picture... You will have a clear field, my friend, a clear field."

Smith nodded, but he wasn't convinced.

"I'll let you know as soon as I get word that the SSN-S1 has been sunk," Tosenko said, clapping his hand on Smith's shoulder. "Boxer is dead, only he doesn't know it. But he will, I guarantee, he will!"

Boxer studied the sonar display. The three targets, already ID'd as Russian Kotkin-class frigates: the *Bravyy*, *Veskiy* and the *Svetlyy*. The three were twenty-five miles away, off St. Lawrence Island, at the southern end of the Bering Strait. The three were moving in parallel formation with eight thousand yards between them.

"According to NAVSYS, we're going to be in only seventy feet of water soon," Stark said. He was standing behind Boxer, and slightly to his right.

"It's been so easy up to now ... well, I just want to get the job done with, and go home," Boxer said.

"It seldom works that way," Stark answered.

Boxer rubbed his chin, now bristling with several days growth, because he decided one morning that he was tired of shaving... The truth was he was tired of everything, and if it wasn't that this mission was a matter of *life or death* for the world's oceans, he would have gone off somewhere to find himself...

"They know where we are, just as we know where they are," Stark commented.

Boxer moved several steps to the right, and switched on the Weather Data Readout. It took less than two minutes for the golfball-size instrument package to be released, float to the surface, and immediately begin transmitting the data in code. This was decoded as soon as it was received, and displayed on the weather monitor.

"Okay, they have heavy seas, and frigid temperatures... A Force 7 storm blowing... That's going to give us some edge, but not a hell of a lot... We'll make a run through them... Their skippers will know it, but they'll have a hard time keeping up with us, once we're past them."

"What about *getting* past them?" Stark asked.

"We sure as hell will know it if we *don't* make it, won't we?" Boxer asked, keeping his face expressionless.

"I'm glad to see that you're back to your old self again," Stark answered.

Boxer nodded, went back to the Captain's chair, and sounded battle stations on the klaxon.

SSN-S1 moved at flank speed through the frigid waters of the Bering Strait.

"Bottom, five feet," a man at the fathometer called out.

Boxer checked the bottom UWIS scan. The sea floor was strewn with huge boulders, that could easily tear a gash in the boat's hull.

"Targets, bearing zero five... Range, five thousand yards... Speed, ten knots... Course, three five zero," the SO reported.

Suddenly, the dreaded pinging of the Russian sonar filled the SSN-S1.

"They're ranging on us," Sarkis said.

"Rig for depth charges," Boxer announced over the 1MC. To Sarkis he said, "Come to course, six zero."

"Course, six zero," Sarkis answered, moving the rudder control dial on the NAVSYS.

The pinging stopped.

"Bottom, ten feet," the fathometer operator reported.

Boxer's eyes went to the bottom-scanning UWIS. A large crevasse was beginning to show on the monitor.

"SO, go to a cosecant square scan," Boxer said.

"Cosecant square scan," the SO reported.

"Look at that lovely crack!" Boxer exclaimed, as the rift on the sea floor became clearer on the sonar display, then on the UWIS.

"My God, that's even more beautiful —"

"Don't say it," Boxer laughed, "because right now it certainly is more beautiful than any crack you, or I, or any man aboard has seen in a long, long while! DO, make two hundred."

"Making two hundred," the DO answered.

The SSN-S1 slipped into the crevasse.

"It's going to take the Russians a while to find us again," Boxer said.

"Do you think any of our own ships are looking for us?" Sarkis asked.

"I hope not," Boxer answered, and gave his attention to the UWIS display. The rift ran in a north-south direction, and as the SSN-S1 moved through it, it became wider.

Suddenly, the SO reported that the three Russian ships had separated, and were now using skip-dipping tactics.

Boxer checked the sonar display. The frigates were moving in a pattern that suggested a circle, with the SSN-S1 as its center.

"Make sixty feet," Boxer ordered.

"Making sixty feet," the DO answered.

"They know where we are," Boxer said tightly.

"Once they start using ASROCS, we can be trapped in that crevasse, sunk by the falling rock."

Suddenly, the SO reported, "Targets, incoming five four, three six, closing fast."

"Helm, hard left," Boxer said, getting to his feet.

"Helm, hard left," Sarkis answered.

The two ASROCS passed under them, and exploded against the side of the crevasse.

"We should be off the continental shelf in an hour," Boxer said. "Once we're in deep water, we'll have room to maneuver."

Boxer played a game of cat and mouse with the three frigates, changing course as many as a half-dozen times within a ten-minute period, to prevent the Russian from echo-ranging on the SSN-S1.

The control room was absolutely silent, except for the commands necessary to operate the boat.

Boxer was as tense as he ever was in a combat situation. Several time he had the opportunity for a clear shot at one or another of the frigates, but did not order any of the torpedoes fired.

"Bottom, three hundred feet, and falling off," the fathometer operator called out.

"We're homing in on our target!" Boxer exclaimed. "Activate monitors."

"Radiation monitors activated," Stark responded.

"Arm minisubs."

"Minisubs armed," a junior officer responded.

"Radiation increasing," Stark said.

"Get a fix on source," Boxer ordered.

"Radiation, bearing zero four, range, twenty miles, depth, two thousand feet."

"Activate minisubs' NAVSYS."

Quickly and efficiently, the crew of the SSN-S1 went through the procedures necessary to launch and control the minisubs to their targets.

"Stand by to launch minisubs," Boxer ordered.

"Standing by," the launch officer replied. "Bays one and two flooded. Doors open."

"Start power," Boxer said.

"Power on... Launch completed," the launch officer reported. "Bay doors closed. Pumps activated."

"All right, Stark, get those babies to their target," Boxer said.

"ETA ten minutes," Stark reported from the radio control panel. "All systems go... Looking good on the UWIS."

"Stand by to surface," Boxer announced over the 1MC. "All hands, stand by to surface." Just as he was about hit the klaxon button, a tremendous explosion lifted the boat upwards.

Boxer grabbed the side of the chair.

"Target, bearing one seven five, range, fifteen miles, depth, six hundred feet, course, forty."

"Come to course, four five."

"Coming to course, four five," Sarkis reported.

Boxer switched on the SYSTEST NET. All systems were green.

"Minisubs on target," Stark reported.

Boxer hit the klaxon button to signal that the boat was surfacing.

One of the phones rang.

Sarkis answered. "We're taking water in the aft torpedo room," he reported.

"How much?"

"The SO recommends evacuating the men, and sealing off the section."

"Do it."

"Passing through one foot," the DO reported. "Minisubs—"

Two huge explosions shook the SSN-S1.

"Target destroyed," Stark announced.

"Fifty feet," the DO reported.

"Bridge detail, stand by," Boxer ordered.

"Standing by," the Master Chief answered.

"COMMO, radio Headquarters on an open frequency: Mission accomplished, Admiral Jack Boxer and crew," Boxer said with a smile. Then he added, "I feel good!"

A NOTE TO THE READER

Dear Reader,

If you have enjoyed the novel enough to leave a review on **Amazon** and **Goodreads**, then we would be truly grateful.

Sapere Books

Sapere Books is an exciting new publisher of brilliant fiction and popular history.

To find out more about our latest releases and our monthly bargain books visit our website: **saperebooks.com**